The President's Jeep stopped instantly,

and Secret Service men pulled the President and national security adviser out of the Jeep and hustled them into the dense trees. The security professionals, in well-rehearsed routine, spread out away from the road to avoid bombs or snipers in case the trees were the opening salvo of an ambush.

The Secret Service moved the President and adviser continually through the trees, circling, never stopping long enough to give a rifleman a steady target.

Under most situations, the evasion techniques would have been highly successful.

Gunfire suddenly ripped through the trees.

The national security adviser was blasted forward, his spine shattered, his cheerful face stretched in death's horror . . .

NICK CARTER IS IT!

"Nick Carter out-Bonds James Bond."
>—*Buffalo Evening News*

"Nick Carter is America's #1 espionage agent."
>—*Variety*

"Nick Carter is razor-sharp suspense."
>—*King Features*

"Nick Carter has attracted an army of addicted readers . . . the books are fast, have plenty of action and just the right degree of sex . . . Nick Carter is the American James Bond, suave, sophisticated, a killer with both the ladies and the enemy."

>—*New York Times*

FROM THE NICK CARTER
KILLMASTER SERIES

NICK CARTER

KILLMASTER

The Execution Exchange

C

CHARTER BOOKS, NEW YORK

THE EXECUTION EXCHANGE

A Charter Book/published by arrangement with
The Condé Nast Publications, Inc.

PRINTING HISTORY
Charter Original/November 1985

ISBN: 0-441-21877-6

Charter Books are published by The Berkley Publishing Group,
200 Madison Avenue, New York, New York 10016.
PRINTED IN THE UNITED STATES OF AMERICA

*Dedicated to the men of the
Secret Services of the
United States of America*

PROLOGUE

The cool night air smelled of smoke, expensive liquor, and power. Senators, congressmen, and Cabinet members exchanged pleasantries with disenchanted wives and hungry lobbyists in the manicured backyard of a red-brick Georgetown mansion. Occasionally there was a real conversation.

"Defense's stench is rising to the rafters, Mark," said the man smoking the long cheroot. His eyes roamed the crowd, stopping now and then to assess a particularly beautiful aspiring Washington hostess. "You've really done it. MXs, AWACS recon jets, and that blasted secret Krobel gas. I'm surprised the Israelis will put up with it, even if it is to correct the mistakes in Beirut."

"Gentlemen?" The waiter in white tie and tails held up the silver tray with two drinks.

"It's a matter of logistics," the secretary of defense said mildly. He took the long-stemmed martini glass from the tray and gazed at the clear liquid. He'd learned to survive in Washington by speaking and acting slowly. It made him appear thoughtful.

"Logistics, bah!" said the man with the cigar. He drank the Old Fashioned in a gulp, then put it back on the tray.

"Your brother-in-law's plastics firm will make at least a million in the next month on your Beirut orders!"

The secretary of defense's face paled. He drank deeply from his martini and waved away the waiter before he heard more.

"Malcolm . . . you won't print . . ."

A broad smile spread across the reporter's face.

"You can bet on it," he said and smoked his cheroot with pleasure. "Every last dirty detail . . ."

The reporter stopped, staring at the peculiar expression on the secretary's face.

The older man swayed. His martini glass smashed onto the bricked patio. He tore at the stiff collar at his throat and collapsed gasping beside the glass.

The reporter's shout for help stilled the gaiety in that corner of the patio. While solemn-faced partygoers crowded around the dying secretary of defense, the waiter in white tie and tails handed his silver tray to a startled guest and hurried into the mansion.

As the waiter walked, he pulled a sheet of folded stationery from his inside pocket and smoothed it against his chest. Quickly, efficiently, knowing as a waiter he wouldn't be questioned at this exclusive private party, he tacked it to the outside of the massive front door. He smiled triumphantly. The timing had been perfect. He slipped off into the starry night.

Four of the five men wore dark three-piece suits and shined wing-tip shoes. The fifth man—the Vice-President of the United States—wore crisp trousers, an open-necked white shirt with the sleeves rolled up, and alligator loafers. His marketing people had advised him that this casual attire told voters he was a hard worker but approachable, a man to be trusted with a problem. His trademark clothes had been convincing voters to elect him to various offices for twenty-four years. It didn't seem to matter that he was also good at his job. He'd learned that it was enough for him that he cared.

Now he sat in a high-backed chair in a Washington, D.C., hotel conference room facing the four businessmen in their regimental dark suits. Three filled the long sofa, and the fourth had taken up a nearby chair. The ashtrays were full. Empty beer and soda cans overflowed the plastic wastebasket. Outside, beyond the drawn blinds, heavy nighttime traffic droned.

"You owe us," the Vice-President said patiently again as if explaining to stubborn children. "You owe us plenty for that last tax cut. You're raking in the dough. Now it's dues time. The boss wants the strike over before Congress opens, before the opposition pushes through a tough prolabor bill."

The three businessmen on the sofa growled and muttered to one another while the fourth businessman in the nearby chair watched. At last he nodded thoughtfully.

"Go take a leak, Jeff," he told the Vice-President. "I want to talk to the boys. Maybe we can work something out."

"Right."

The Vice-President stood and hitched his trousers. He'd risen to power through the back rooms of Chicago and Washington. He knew when victory was on the horizon. The President would be pleased.

As the businessmen watched silently, the Vice-President strode into the hallway where his aides and Secret Service protectors waited. He nodded briskly to reassure them, then walked down the corridor toward the john.

The masked man was waiting behind the stairwell door. Abruptly he stepped to the edge of the corridor.

The Vice-President recoiled.

The assassin opened fire.

The Vice-President went down, a Secret Service man on top of him. Instantly other Secret Service men fired in return. They had no choice.

The assassin fell, his chest ripped into a pulpy mass, blood splattering onto the white hallway walls.

"Christ!" the Vice-President shouted. "Who is he?"

Doors along the corridor burst open in the sudden quiet. The Vice-President's aides rushed to him. He stood, unharmed but bloody from the wounded arm of the Secret Service man who'd saved his life.

"Anything on him?" the Vice-President asked, his voice shaking.

One of the Secret Service men kneeling beside the assassin took a heavy, high-quality piece of rag bond stationery from the assassin's hip pocket. He unfolded it and read.

"I think this may be useful, sir."

He handed it to the Vice-President.

As the helicopter landed under the star-studded sky, the President and the national security adviser stared down at the small, well-lit pad. Between the circle of lights and the perimeter of mountain firs, shadows of Secret Service men stood unmoving and alert, rifles over their arms. It was the massive security customary for all presidents, even at this top-secret, isolated retreat.

"No telephones," the national security adviser murmured in awe. "No crazies, reporters, or angry taxpayers."

The President laughed.

"Getting to you, Richard? Well, we'll get some work done here. You can only commune with nature so long."

The helicopter blades singing overhead, the two government officials and their aides jumped onto the pad and were escorted by the watchful Secret Service to waiting Jeeps.

The asphalt-covered road wound up and around the mountain. The Jeep's headlights swept the dark, shadowy trees at each curve.

"Is that fence electrified?" the national security adviser asked curiously as their Jeep sped past.

"And patrolled," the President said. "The biggest challenge around here is to take a walk alone."

The road grew bumpy, the left side washed out. A barricade warned vehicles away where the road was being repaired during the day.

As the stars twinkled through the waving tree branches, the two men sat in grateful, tired silence, happily depending on the expert driver who pushed the Jeep on up the steep mountainside.

A tree had fallen across the road. It was a big fir that completely blocked passage. The lead Jeep skidded to a stop. Walkie-talkies crackled.

The President's Jeep stopped instantly, and Secret Service men pulled the President and national security adviser out of the Jeep and hustled them into the dense trees. The security professionals, in well-rehearsed routine, spread out away from the road to avoid bombs or snipers in case the tree were the opening salvo of an ambush.

As three men crept back to check around the downed fir, the rest of the Secret Service moved the President and adviser continually through the trees, circling, never stopping long enough to give a rifleman a steady target.

Under most situations, the evasion techniques would have been highly successful.

Gunfire suddenly ripped through the trees.

The national security adviser was blasted forward, his spine shattered, his cheerful face stretched in death's horror.

Two of the Secret Service men grabbed the President and threw him under a nearby Jeep. Others dropped to their knees, looking for targets. Whoever the attackers were, they had known exactly what the Secret Service would do. Desperate, the Secret Service shot blindly at the branches where they thought they'd seen fire.

It was enough. Two bodies fell from branches. Shots from both sides reverberated in the forest.

In five minutes, the battle was over. The stench of cordite burned the President's nostrils. He crawled out from under the Jeep. Four of his men had been wounded. Besides the two assassins who'd fallen from the branches, two more were dead. One was shot by the President's men, the other a suicide from some poison, not a mark on him.

The President surveyed the bloody scene and saw the body of the national security adviser. As he rushed to him, four Secret Service men discovered printed documents nailed to trees. They snatched them off, studied them briefly, then—shaken—took them to the President.

Even at midnight, officers and servicemen filled the long, cool Pentagon corridors. They carried papers or rifles, walking briskly as they routinely fulfilled their jobs. The tired ones were coming off duty. Others with spring in their steps were on their way to relieve their posts. The Pentagon never slept, but tonight the big complex seemed insomniac. There was too much activity. Something big was going on. Something big, terrifying, and highly secret.

Inside a soundproof, electronically safe conference room, coffee percolated quietly in an alcove. Five somber men and women stood in a semicircle around a portable magnetic bulletin board. On the board were displayed the six documents from the assassinations and attempted assassinations that had happened simultaneously that same night.

FBI and CIA experts had X-rayed the documents' expensive paper and checked thoroughly for fingerprints and poisonous substances. They had analyzed the printing inks, researched the typefaces, and computerized the arrangements of words.

"Nothing!" said the tall thin man with a scar down his left cheek. Fear and worry mixed in his cultured voice. "So ordinary . . . so common that even the paper could have been bought at any corner stationery store."

"What about area printers?" said a woman. She had graying hair styled in a fluffy crown. At other times she wore the glossy hair saucily, proud of the color that age had earned. But tonight the hair seemed limp, lifeless, as if her comprehension of the recent violence had sapped her life force. "Aren't there any blips in the typeface we can track to one particular machine?"

"It's laser printed," the man with the scar said simply. "In Washington, any decent-size office is going to have a word processor and laser printer. Perfect reproduction."

"You have to hand it to them," mused another man as he stroked his beard with trembling fingers. "They've put a lot of detailed work into the design. Legal judgments."

"*Not* legal. Congress would have to bring them first. They're judgments that find the President, Vice-President, secretary of defense, and national security adviser guilty of crimes against the world!" said the woman. She stalked toward the coffeepot, an empty cup in her hand. "They only *appear* legal. What gall! Guilty!"

"Which terrorist gang?" muttered a second woman, her hands clasped behind her back. She intently studied the documents as if by sheer will she could force them to answer her questions. "Which country?"

There was a loud thud on the door.

"Yes?" said the man with the scar.

The door opened, and the Vice-President strode in. He

wore a rumpled suit jacket over his traditional white shirt. His face was pale. Flecks of blood had dried in his white-templed hair.

"What do you have?" he asked, taking the cup of coffee the woman at the urn poured for him.

As the security experts talked, the coffee cooled in his hand. When they'd finished, he put down the cup and picked up the red phone on the conference table. There was no device for dialing. The telephone connected directly to the President.

"Yes, sir," the Vice-President said and related what he'd learned. "Not much information. The assassins were highly trained and experienced, but unknown to any agents we have contacts with in the world. No clues, sir."

The Vice-President listened grimly. At last he laid the receiver in the cradle and looked up at the worried group surrounding him.

"The President says to get Hawk. He'll know what to do."

ONE

Admirers call Budapest the Little Paris on the Danube. From ancient Buda's castled hills on the river's west bank to the more contemporary Pest's wide boulevards on the east, native Hungarians and impressed tourists daily crossed and recrossed Budapest's eight graceful bridges to visit government offices, restaurants, concert halls, coffeehouses, cabarets, and casinos. The locations were not merely attractive, but exuded as much worldly charm as the best of other European capitals.

Nick Carter reflected on this as he drove a taxi through Pest's boulevards of worn paving stones, following his quarry—a dangerous double agent whose recent discovery would, AXE hoped, result soon in his capture or at least death before he did any more harm.

Twilight spread inky fingers thick into the sky. A dying ruby haze hung on the horizon. And in the old street alongside Carter, cars built in East Germany, Poland, Romania, and the Soviet Union competed with Czechoslovak streetcars and Hungarian buses for noisy, smoke-belching space on the Great Hungarian Plain. The Warsaw Pact nation was rooted to the past with her architectural and

9

historical treasures while the present bustled importantly in her streets.

The double agent drove a small blue Russian Lada. He turned corners and waited at traffic lights, apparently a law-abiding citizen. Carter, N3 with America's ultrasecret agency AXE, pursued expertly in his AXE-supplied taxicab. He attracted no attention. In his open-necked white shirt and faded Levi's he was just another moonlighting Hungarian, one of the vast hidden economy of workers making do in a communist nation. His only difference was the intensity of his cool, flinty eyes. They constantly moved. He missed nothing. His life and mission depended on it.

A panel truck with vegetables painted on the side pulled in front of Carter. Quickly the American agent looked past it.

As Carter suspected, the double agent's Lada, ahead in the next lane, swerved. The small blue car shot down a narrow side street in escape.

Instantly Carter pressed the accelerator, and his yellow taxi cut into the lane.

The panel truck speeded up, angling sharply in front of Carter, trying to force him to the curb.

Vehicles on the boulevard honked.

Carter rammed his bumper into the side of the panel truck. The side street was just ahead.

The truck bounced, scraped, then steadied. It wove back and forth, blocking two lanes to stop Carter's pursuit.

Drivers honked and stuck their heads out their windows to yell insults.

Carter stuck his head out too. He yelled like the others. But in his hand was Wilhelmina, his perfectly bored 9mm Luger. In the noise and confusion, he shot twice. The panel truck's rear tires exploded. No one noticed.

The truck lumbered slowly on, the remains of its tires slapping the paving stones.

Carter once more pressed the taxi's accelerator. He skill-fully slipped between the lanes of traffic. The honking and Hungarian insults increased.

The panel truck tried to swerve.

But Carter burst past the laboring vehicle, around a Porsche, and down the busy side street where the quarry's Lada had disappeared.

Lighted businesses lined the narrow, one-block-long street. People walked briskly on the sidewalks, carrying packages and loaves of bread. There was no sign of the Lada.

Carter sped on, weaving among the vehicles, the panel truck growing smaller in his rearview mirror as it gamely tried to pursue.

Suddenly the blue Lada darted out of the traffic ahead. It angled right and disappeared.

Carter's sharp eyes followed the movement. Had the car gone down an alley?

He pushed the taxi on, watching the glass-fronted stores, offices, and blank apartments that formed a solid wall to the end of the block. No alleyway.

Then he saw it. The enormous flat door of a downtown mechanic's garage. If open, the entrance would be ample for the small Lada to race in and skid to a stop.

Carter pulled the steering wheel left and parked toward the end of the block. The quarry—and those who protected him—had identified the taxi. But perhaps they still hadn't identified Carter.

He got out and put on a black jacket of cheap fabric worn shiny with age. With the jeans, he was dressed like the other modern Hungarian males around him. The uniform varied with plaid shirts and sneakers, but the basics were still West-ern jeans and Eastern jacket. The communists didn't approve of the mix, but the crushed Hungarian revolution in 1956 had eventually reaped a few liberties.

"Number Fourteen Józsefhegyi Street on Rose Hill," the deep Hungarian voice told Carter.

"Sorry," Carter said, turning toward the man. "Off duty."

The man looked up, his hand on the taxi's back door handle.

"Only a short run," the tall, rangy man said. "Double the fare."

"Maybe later," Carter said, watching the man curiously. He'd given an address in the most fashionable neighborhood in Budapest. He could be an important artist or government official, or he could be an agent with a transparent cover.

The man had a long, boneless face, expressionless as if he had no thoughts. He nodded slowly. Another idea occurred to Carter. Maybe somebody wanted Carter to know the tall man was an agent.

"I understand," the man said and walked away.

Carter watched, already delayed perhaps too long. At last the man disappeared. No one was taking particular notice of Carter. He strode across the street to the three-story garage. A wind off the Danube whipped at his jacket.

No lights showed at the garage. On one side of the building was a bright, customer-filled hat and glove store. On the other was a butcher shop with pink hams and sausages hanging in the window. Between the butcher shop and the garage was a steep, dark stairway. A closed pedestrian door was between that and the massive garage door. There was no sound from inside the garage.

He looked up and down the street, then tried the pedestrian door into the garage. The knob turned.

His other hand on the Luger under his jacket, he opened the door a crack. Faint light showed distantly within.

Again he checked for watchful eyes on the street around him, then he drew the Luger and slipped into the garage, flat against the wall.

The blue Lada was parked about fifteen feet inside the door. It was empty. A naked bulb glowed an invitation at the end of the long, two-story room. It illuminated a double-doored elevator. Shadowy cars and motorcycles were parked at angles against the wall, waiting for their repairs to be finished by invisible garagemen. The air smelled of grease, gas, and emptiness.

The hairs on the back of Carter's neck stood.

He knew it was a trap, but he had to go on. He had an assignment to fulfill.

On silent cat feet, he crept around the perimeter of the room.

A grease gun fell clattering to the concrete floor.

He froze, looking down at the tool. It was slippery, and had been left on the workbench uncleaned. Either the mechanic was sloppy, or he was in a big hurry.

Carter resumed his quiet approach. Outside traffic sounds were muffled and distant. A chill hung in the high-ceilinged empty room.

At last he reached the elevator. There was no inside staircase. No other way to go up or down. Or was there?

Suddenly he understood.

He pressed the lever that would call the cage down. The men waiting above expected Carter to get on. They would be ready for him on the third floor with guns and saps, and he didn't want them to get restless. Not yet.

He ran softly back across the garage floor, past the work-benches and cars. He slipped out the pedestrian door to the sidewalk and stood motionless in traffic-made shadows that wavered against the garage's wall.

Soon he heard what he'd expected: the liberated footsteps of a man who thought he'd lost his tail.

The double agent.

Carter blended deep into the shadows at the side of the garage's big flat door.

The quarry stepped lightly from the outside staircase onto the sidewalk. He glanced casually around, his gaze sweeping the busy night. He reached inside his jacket.

Carter's grip tightened on his Luger, but the double agent drew out only a pack of Bulgarian cigarettes.

He reflected on the double agent's stupidity as the man cupped his hands around a match and lit the cigarette. In the process, he illuminated his rough, spoiled face long enough for anyone along the congested street to memorize it. The man had seen too many spy movies and romanticized his work.

The quarry blew out the match and flicked it down to the sidewalk. He turned abruptly, dismissing the safe but uninteresting street, and strode away.

Keeping to the shadows, using the remarkable training and intellect that had kept him alive and made him the top Killmaster, Carter followed. By the relaxed shoulders of his quarry, the American agent knew the other man was now convinced his tail had been lured upstairs to the garage's offices and eliminated. He was safe, and proud of the clever subterfuge that had killed his pursuer.

The quarry walked a quarter mile, weaving in and out of crowds, crossing thronged streets, passing offices, businesses, and restaurants exuding the spicy smells of pig livers, paprika, brown bread, fried cutlets, sausages, pickles, and törkoly, a traditional Hungarian brandy made from the skins of grapes after they'd been crushed for wine.

The Hungarian regularly checked his watch. He walked faster. His seasoned gaze roamed the horizon.

At last the double agent reached the wide Danube, its wet smell fresh in the air. Carter followed closely now. The river was black and deep in the closing night. Excursion boats at the landing docks were strung with small sparkling lights. Gypsy violins sang haunting melodies. A great shiny tourist bus from Austria drove up to one dock and unloaded tourists in evening dress for an expensive dinner.

The quarry continued on, heedless. He was late. He'd abandoned his Lada for the safety of his feet. Several times he almost broke into a run as he crossed the bridge into Buda. Now he was worried. Whoever he was meeting was important . . . or terrifying.

The soaring, graceful figure at the top of the liberation monument came into view against the starry sky. The double agent climbed Gellért Hill two steps at a time, and Carter followed.

Here the eleventh-century Venetian missionary Bishop Gellért was martyred. Carter considered this. Now the hill was a verdant park overlooking the city, and at the top was the Citadel, a hotel, wine cellar, café, and the statue commemorating the Soviet troops' victory over the Germans in 1945. Because of that success, Budapest had been liberated, turned communist, and was now after thirty years slowly, inexorably moving toward the profit motive and private ownership. From martyrdom to a glimmer of freedom after eight hundred years of servitude to other nations. Carter shook his head sadly.

The double agent paused at a stone wall. Carter turned his back, pretending to study the monument. Beyond it, beautiful nighttime Budapest spread in a festival of twinkling lights.

From the corners of his eyes, he watched the double agent carefully take in the few nighttime sightseers.

Satisfied, the double agent vaulted the stone wall and disappeared in the shadows of tall, overhanging trees.

Quickly Carter strode along the wall. Satisfied that the position was good, he too leaped over into the small forest. From tree to tree, he closed in on low, whispered voices.

There were two men, and one of them he recognized from

the voice tape he'd heard in a secret AXE briefing room three days ago. It was definitely his quarry, the double agent.

He held his Luger, felt the balance, and circled closer to the voices.

They weren't speaking Hungarian.

At last Carter saw them, two average-size figures in filtered starlight at arm's length from one another. The double agent was rubbing his palms nervously along his pants, and now Carter knew why. He smiled.

The language was Romanian.

And the other man was General Carol Romanescu, chief of the Romanian secret police and powerful member of the Romanian Politburo. Causing his displeasure was enough to make any man sweat.

Suddenly a third figure leaped down silently from a tree.

Carter raced forward.

The figure fell on Romanescu.

Before the Romanian could roll away, before Carter could get there, the figure's hand shot up. A knife's long blade glinted briefly. The sharp steel plunged deep into Romanescu's heart.

TWO

The killer was dressed all in black. He'd been waiting in the tree's branches for the meeting between the double agent and the leader of the Romanian secret police. But waiting to kill only Carol Romanescu.

Nick Carter lunged down the incline.

Frantic, the Hungarian double agent searched Romanescu's jacket pockets for the information he'd just turned over.

The killer, his face hidden in shadows, calmly pulled out his knife from Romanescu's chest. His assignment was over. He turned away.

Carter threw himself at the two.

The killer bolted.

The Hungarian double agent jumped up, papers clutched in one hand, a Walther aimed at Carter's heart in the other.

"Killmaster!" the Hungarian growled, surprised. "Lousy Killmaster. You're dead!"

"You always were a wishful thinker, József."

Two bullets rang out from the Walther.

One bullet whistled past Carter, just missing his ear. The second went where aimed—into the double agent's papers. The sheaf exploded into a falling ball of flame and ash just as Carter hit József's midsection. The papers had been chemi-

17

cally treated for quick disposal before the wrong eyes saw them.

József gasped for air, then jammed a knife at Carter.

Carter swiveled, kicking the knife. Too late to help the dead Romanescu, it landed in the crook of the Romanian leader's arm, blade pointed toward the stars.

In the distance, the wail of police sirens grew through the night. A good citizen had reported the gunshots on Gellért Hill.

"Give up, József. You can buy your life with information."

"You cheap Westerners! You'd ruin my standard of living."

The double agent quickly aimed the Walther.

But before he could fire, Carter slapped it from his hand and sent a slashing punch to his jaw.

The Hungarian's face stretched with surprise and fear as he helplessly crashed back through the air. As if he'd practiced for hours, he landed perfectly on top of the dead Romanian.

The knife blade that was balanced against Romanescu sliced neatly between the double agent's back ribs. It punctured his heart. He grunted and his eyes snapped open.

"*Nem!*" he shouted. "No!"

The eyes froze open. Death's glaze quickly set in.

The police sirens close upon him, Carter raced off after the killer in black.

It was the man in the white shirt and dark sports jacket who was tying the black sweater around his neck that attracted Carter's attention. The man was strolling across the shadowy plaza on Gellért Hill, the sweater hanging down his back from his shoulders while he knotted the limp arms low under his chin. When the man reached the railing, he stopped, grasped it with both hands, and then leaned forward like any eager tourist to better soak up the diamondlike glow of beautiful Budapest at night.

He seemed not to notice the sirens.

Carter smiled. The killer. A thrifty, confident killer who couldn't throw even his disguise away—a good black sweater big enough when worn to hide a white shirt and the standard Hungarian jacket.

The AXE agent turned, whistled soundlessly, and stared off over another railing at the black Danube while he watched in his peripheral vision the figure of the killer.

The killer was delaying—either trying to figure out whether anyone had spotted him, or waiting to meet a contact.

Below, police cars with revolving red lights screeched to a halt.

Ahead of Carter, the full moon spread its silvery light in a path down the center of the Danube. Carter watched the expanding ripples until at last the killer turned and sauntered away down the steps. The man was wary, so Carter waited until he was almost out of sight.

As policemen ran up the steps, their guns drawn, the AXE agent descended.

The killer glanced up and down the street, then walked quickly to a green Renault parked at the curb near the police cars. He unlocked the door, got in, and started the motor. Carter had yet to get a look at his face. There was something disturbingly familiar about his walk.

The American agent watched for a taxi, but the evening streets were at last quieting, citizens and tourists gone to homes and hotels searching for dinners and rest.

Carter could take the killer now, could break the window and shove the Luger in the killer's face, but he wanted to know why the man had killed Romanescu and not the double agent as well. Had he only wanted to kill? He hadn't been after the papers. Carter needed to follow the killer, to get information for Hawk.

Still some distance away, the American agent circled the Hungarian police cars and the officer left to guard them. He slouched, then ran toward the Renault.

As the green sedan took off, Carter stepped onto the back bumper, wrapped his muscled hands over the chrome, and crouched for the ride.

The sedan journeyed through the streets of medieval Buda and into Pest. Other drivers' mouths fell open. Sometimes they pointed and honked. But the killer kept on, his puzzled face occasionally turning from side to side. People don't see what they can't conceive.

The killer slowed the vehicle. A rococo hotel filled the block. Carter hopped off the bumper and walked to a magazine stand next to a granite wall still pocked by gunfire from the unsuccessful 1956 revolt.

As the killer parked, the AXE agent bought a Soviet newspaper. Four Russian divisions were stationed in Hungary. Like soldiers all over the world, they wanted to know what they were missing at home.

Carter turned, and saw the edge of the black sweater disappear inside the double doors of the massive hotel. He counted to ten, then followed.

The hotel's foyer was three stories high, glittering with gold leaf, painted with pastel colors. People walked softly down the wide staircases, their voices subdued in awe by the unusual aura of privilege and wealth. The distinct classes that made wealth and privilege not only possible but inevitable in Hungary had been destroyed by the Soviets after they liberated the nation in 1945. Instead, the communists substituted communal guilt. Landowners were called pretentious peasants, and intellectuals were vultures serving fascism. Once beaten down to a common, low economic and intellectual level, Hungarians knew that whatever they'd done in the past was wrong. The drab future was one of selflessness dedicated to serving the state. Personal wishes were not only unimportant, they were dangerous. Then came the bloody revolt in 1956 and a slow but steady return to individual as well as communal interests. Repression called by any name always led to revolution.

Carter thought about this as he followed the killer through corridors past elaborate dining rooms and enormous meeting halls celebrating the past. Even an unsuccessful revolution often won eventually. No government could hold down its people forever.

And then the killer was gone. Disappeared.

The corridor was crowded with talking, laughing waiters and waitresses in black and white uniforms. The waiters pushed food-laden carts and carried silver buckets of ice. They jostled past Carter toward the dining and meeting rooms he'd just passed. The waitresses wore modest knee-length skirts, bright red lipstick, and carried trays covered with champagne glasses.

Ahead, wide doors swung back and forth, showing a bustling kitchen that sparkled with chrome, copper, and shiny white paint. The smells of baking meats and pastries wafted out. Inside, chefs in tall white hats held court, shouting, cursing, swinging ladles or knives over their heads in emphasis.

Carefully, quickly checking around him, Carter moved against the flow and into the kitchen.

"Out of my way!" complained a sous chef, deliberately shouldering Carter as he hurried past with an oversize kettle.

"No visitors!" shouted another as he glared over a string of peppers.

"Who is this man?" boomed the authoritative voice of the Hungarian head chef. "Get him out of here! I won't have my dinners ruined!"

"Pardon," said Carter as he weaved past the gleaming counters and mounds of fresh vegetables. "A friend. I'm looking for a friend. Did a stranger come in?"

"Only you!" thundered the incensed head chef.

Carter's eyes never stopped moving. The chef was lying. The killer in black had nowhere else to go. He had to have come into the kitchen. The angry, suspicious faces of the chefs and their assistants followed Carter as he at last exited through a door at the back.

He stopped and listened. He was in a long, quiet concrete corridor lined with boxes of kitchen supplies. The din of the kitchen was behind him. A parking lot waited ahead at the end of the corridor.

He padded forward, his ears prickling.

Then he heard the sound.

Leather on cement.

He dropped, rolling forward out the door.

A flash of white shirt and black jacket hurtled past.

The smells of exhaust and rubber stank in the air. Car motors turned over. Wheels squealed. A busy parking garage.

He leaped to his feet and turned, fists raised.

"David!"

"Nick?"

The two men looked deep into one another's eyes and years passed in shock waves between them.

"Why did you kill Romanescu?" Carter said softly.

"I never suspected it was you . . ."

Sir David Sutton gasped. The deep lines on his face twisted. He grabbed his chest and started to collapse.

Carter caught him and carried him behind an old Mercedes

limousine. He laid his former comrade gently on the concrete, wadded the sweater, and slipped it under his head.

He checked the older man's pulse. It was faint and uneven. The breathing was shallow. The closed eyelids were almost translucent.

Age and illness had changed Sutton radically in the ten years since Carter had last seen him, and he had difficulty connecting this sick man with the robust agent he'd worked with and known well. A British hero from World War II, Victoria Cross, the kind of man you wanted beside you on a dangerous mission. And just ten years ago they'd shared several missions.

"Sorry, old boy." Sir David opened his eyes. "Doesn't hurt a bit now." He smiled. "Nice chase. Wish I could play it to the end. The old ticker, you know. Knew it'd fail me just when I needed it."

"Rest, David. I'll get an ambulance."

"Too late, lad. Tell Andrea for me. No blasted strangers."

"David!"

Sir David Sutton sighed and closed his eyes. His lungs expelled a last blast of air.

Carter stayed quietly beside him, memories floating through his mind. At last he squeezed the dead man's shoulder, stood, and walked away.

The telephone number was secret. It led to a contact who passed Carter on to another who again passed Carter on. At last he was given the number he needed. It was a number that changed once or twice a day.

"Sir David Sutton?" the disembodied voice said cheerfully in a crisp Oxbridge accent. "I'll get his file. You Yanks worry too much. MI5 never loses one of its own."

Carter waited in a dark telephone booth, the bulb unscrewed. Farm trucks rumbled past on the way to the Great

Market Hall of downtown Pest. The trucks were heaped with produce, fresh eggs, milk, and cheese—evidence that Hungary's new economic mechanism was working. The new rules decentralized planning and control, allowed supply and demand to function naturally, and permitted individuals to again accumulate wealth. It was a new face for communism, and was gaining increasing success.

"I've found him," the distant voice said. "Sir David Sutton. Retired 1980 because of cardiopulmonary problems. Bad heart, don't you know."

"And recently?"

"Haven't the foggiest. If he's out there, he's not on a job for us."

THREE

Three blocks away in the café section of Pest, Nick Carter's practiced gaze once again took in the animated on-the-towners, bright tourists, and drab Hungarians with a few extra forints looking for a lively time. One precaution any AXE agent learned early in his or her career was never to stay too long in one place. By the time the agent earns a Killmaster rating, it's an unconscious response.

Satisfied he was drawing no unusual attention, Carter strolled to a different telephone. He had another call to make, and he wasn't longing to make it.

"N3," David Hawk's voice growled in the distance. "I've been waiting. Did you get József and the contact? Is the contraband safe?"

Carter knew he was going to disappoint his boss. He told the brilliant head of AXE what had happened on Gellért Hill and in the parking lot behind the old hotel.

"József Pau and Carol Romanescu," Hawk rumbled from Washington. There was an edge to his voice, the same edge of worry that had followed Carter from Gellért to the cold telephone here on the Pest street. "Didn't know József had gone that high up. What the hell was Sutton doing there?"

"Wish I knew."

"If he'd lived, would he have told you?"

"Only if he'd wanted. And he had the time before he died."

"Damned stubborn man, that Sutton."

"Yes, sir. A good agent."

"That, among other things, is what bothers me," Hawk said.

"I checked with MI5," Carter said. "According to their records, Sutton retired in 1980 because of a weak heart."

"I'd heard that, yes. So he was on his own."

"Or with someone else. Working for them or leading them."

"Did you find any"—Hawk's voice hesitated—"er . . . papers, documents there, N3? Legal-appearing documents? Attached to Romanescu's body, or maybe nailed to trees?"

"The contraband—the papers József gave to Romanescu when they met—burned to ash," Carter said, puzzled. "He ignited the papers with a gunshot. Those were the only documents. Should there have been others?"

In Washington, Hawk was strangely silent. He was considering something, perhaps whether to give Carter certain information. Ultrasecret AXE gave out information only on a need-to-know basis. As he patiently waited, Carter's thoughts returned to the Hungarian revolution and to the sweeping amnesty in 1963 that had at last freed many anticommunists and other captives from the revolution. Forever changed by pain and disillusionment, they returned to communist Hungarian life. The wounds from the 1956 revolution ran deep through the Hungarian soul, cutting it as the Danube sliced Buda from Pest. Carter reflected on this as he tried to unravel the meaning of the three men's meeting—Hungarian József Pau, Romanian Carol Romanescu, and Englishman Sir David Sutton—and perhaps even their deaths.

At last Hawk cleared his throat. There was a sudden snap,

and Carter recognized the sound of his chief's butane lighter. Hawk was lighting one of his ever present foul-smelling cigars. A man of impeccable taste in all else, his humanity showed in his preference for cheap, terrible cigars. In far-off Washington, Hawk let out a noisy blast of cigar smoke.

"There was an attempt last night on the President's life," Hawk said.

"What?"

"And the Vice-President's. The secretary of defense and the national security adviser were both killed."

"A plot?"

"The background check on the killers shows no connection at all. One was a Mafia hit man, another a former Green Beret turned mercenary. The others were a Soviet officer who deserted in Afghanistan, a retired Israeli female spy supposedly on vacation in the United States, and a former peacenik from that sixties commune in Findhorn, Scotland."

"But there was a connection." Carter could feel it in his bones. "Does it have to do with the documents you were asking me about?"

"The assassination attempts were accompanied by legal-looking death warrants. Pinned to trees, on one assassin's body, and on the front door of the Georgetown home where the secretary of defense was poisoned." Hawk's voice was cold as ice. He wasn't just worried; he was deeply afraid. This conspiracy had earthshaking implications if it were as international as it appeared. "Each paper named the specific government official indicted, announced he'd been found guilty, and sentenced him to death for crimes against the world."

Carter and Hawk fell silent, each deep in thought.

Crimes against the world reverberated in Carter's mind. In 1968, twelve years after the brave Hungarian revolt, Russia invaded Czechoslovakia to put down a liberal uprising. Hun-

gary, its dreams of independence less important than its fear
of another Soviet reprisal, sent its army, too. Hungary had
learned its lesson well. It was better to win than to lose, and
the illusion of freedom came with too high a price. It was easy
to say that Hungary had been wrong, but if Hungary had
refused, giant Russia would have retaliated.

"Crimes against the world," Carter repeated somberly.
"Hell! What does it mean this time?"

"That, of course, is what we have to discover."

"You think Romanescu might have been a victim of this
group? That means Sutton—"

"It does indeed. And the papers that József burned to
protect himself might have contained the death warrant. If
Sutton were a conspirator, he'd have left it on the body."

Carter looked out at the festive Pest night. Couples strolled
up the boulevard hand in hand, laughing, sharing secrets. A
group of giggling girls huddled in masses of long hair,
hunched shoulders, and budding adolescence as they swung
headlong down the sidewalk toward a café or youth center.
Parents pushed a baby carriage, the tall thin man straight with
pride, the woman holding his arm as if he were the only real
man in the world. Budapest was just another average city
. . . beautiful and old, yes . . . but populated as were all
others with ordinary people who deserved better. Hungary,
the country that had survived years of oppression, ruled for
centuries by others with little sympathy but much greed, had
turned its back on itself in 1968 when it'd helped its latest
conqueror invade sister Czechoslovakia. How could a nation
move forward into liberty and peace if its people wouldn't
lead?

"I'll go to London then," Carter said. "See Andrea."

"The widow," Hawk said, expelling a blast of cigar
smoke far away. "She was MI5 too."

"Your memory is excellent, sir."

"Almost as good as yours, N3." Hawk cleared his throat after the unaccustomed compliment. "I'll have other people checking elsewhere. Report to me quickly."

"I understand."

Carter hung up the phone and walked into the teeming, music-filled Hungarian night.

London's enormous Heathrow Airport had three terminals to serve its nearly eight million residents and thronging tourists. Handling most of the international traffic to England, the airport shuttled travelers to and from their destinations in the remarkable, cheerfully efficient English way. Airline buses ran to downtown London every fifteen or twenty minutes. Trains arrived and left every four minutes during peak periods and every eight to ten minutes at other times. And rail service to Reading, Woking, and Watford Junction stations was available hourly.

Carrying a simple leather briefcase, dressed in a Bonn three-piece business suit, Carter strode through the brightly lit terminal, past airline counters and car rental desks, among the crowds of passengers and dreamers, the bobbies and pickpockets, the exhausted arrivals and excited departing, all moving, milling, searching for signs to where they were going or only hoped to be going, even to a restroom. The staleness of nervous sweat and overworked air conditioning tainted everything.

He pushed outside, eager for air. He breathed deeply of the fresh London morning. Thin sunrise pinks and yellows glowed on the other side of a pale yellow smog. It was a minor smog, nothing like the famous pea-soupers of the 1950s, the ones that for decades had killed people prone to lung problems and shielded crazed murderers like Jack the Ripper. Then London's clean-air laws had gone into effect, and the mists off the Thames began to glow with clear light, not with bituminous coal particles and carbons. Unfortunately, national laws weren't that effective in deterring homicidal criminals, and international laws were even less effective restraining nations hungry for territory, wealth, and increased power.

Carter sighed. Mankind's greatest enemy was himself. The AXE agent hailed a taxi and gave the driver Andrea and David Sutton's address in Soho in London's West End. He got in the black cab and slammed the door.

In the brash, neon quarter of Soho where London's foreign restaurants clustered in greatest number, Carter paid off the Indian driver with the dour face. The man counted the money carefully, then looked at Carter.

"Keep the change," Carter said.

The driver snapped his fingers shut in a sudden display of violent energy. The face didn't smile, but the muscles had relaxed into interest.

Before the driver started a conversation, Carter picked up his briefcase, nodded an acknowledgment of the cabbie's thanks, got out, and—slapping bumpers in the heavy morning traffic—dodged across the street to the restaurant called the Trojan Horse.

Inside, small statues modeled after Phidias' and Praxiteles' works stood displayed in arched alcoves. A mural of the Parthenon was painted across the back wall. Candles waited to be lit at tables where fresh linen tablecloths were stacked. A cleaning crew of three swept and dusted, preparing for the evening's diners.

"We don't serve breakfast or lunch." The man was swarthy and square. He spoke with a mixed accent, English and Greek.

"Lady Sutton, please." Carter took the gold cigarette case from his inside jacket pocket.

"She's asleep, sir. We open at six tonight."

"She'll want to see me now."

Carter offered one of his monogrammed cigarettes to the man, but he shook his head, his gaze moving uneasily around the room after the cleaning crew. Carter lit his cigarette. The man was a fusser. No one who worked under him would ever do a good enough job, but the jobs that were done under his supervision would be more than good enough for any employer.

"Do yourself a favor," Carter said and handed him the gold case and a twenty-pound note. "Keep the money and take her the case. She'll recognize it. I have information about Sir David."

The man looked at the case, then at Carter's face. He took the money first, then turned on his heel to make the delivery. He'd be fast. He didn't want to leave his crew too long.

Carter smoked, enjoying the smoothness of the custom-blended tobaccos. He relaxed, suddenly aware how close he was to exhaustion. The chases through Budapest, watching David Sutton die, the disturbing information from Hawk, and then the late-night flight to Heathrow. Death and faithlessness were all part of the job, but sometimes even the best, the most experienced agent reached saturation.

"She says to come up," the crew boss told Carter, surprised. "She says you'll understand."

Carter put out his cigarette in a silver ashtray and listened to the man's directions, ignoring the curious eyes, the suspicious tone of voice. Alone, he strode across the dining room, doubled back to the closed-off waiting area at the front of the restaurant near the bar, and then through a side door that opened onto a spiral staircase.

"Nick! How wonderful," she called down, a shimmering blue silk robe wrapped around her as if it were thick enough to hold off the chill London air. "But I didn't expect you.

What an odd hour!''

"Next time I'll make an appointment," he said and smiled up at her as he climbed the fragile staircase.

"I couldn't come down."

"Not dressed yet," he said. "No reason you should be."

"Coffee? Black?"

"You remembered."

"How could I forget."

He followed her across a sunny foyer hung with ferns and ivies and into a bedroom so large that it was probably the same size as the dining room below. There were only the two rooms, and a bath on the far side. The walls were eggshell white, the floor hardwood parquet with rag rugs in the old English style on either side of the bed and then a large one beneath a piecrust coffee table between the two overstuffed sofas.

The bedclothes had been thrown back. The indentation from her sleep formed a shallow, round recess. She handed him the cigarette case, smiled briefly, avoiding his eyes, then went to the fireplace.

"Cold, isn't it?" she said and knelt. "For this time of year."

She struck a match, turned on the gas, and the flames licked high over dry logs. She added another, still kneeling, her bottom round and small beneath the negligee.

"You'll have tea?" he asked.

"Of course. Homer is bringing a tray. Coffee and tea."

She stood again, her back to him. She squared her shoulders and turned. She looked at him.

She had large gray eyes and rich brown hair. The chiseled cheekbones were high, the nose straight and slightly turned up at the end. Her face had a deep glow as if from some internal, unquenchable fire. With no makeup, her hair tousled, and the softness of sleep clinging like perfume, she was a walking invitation for sex. She was almost forty now, the skin beginning to line around the eyes and furrow between the brows, but for her, life always would just be starting.

From the time Carter had known her, she'd been direct and honest, and now she looked at him unflinchingly as if to say she'd done what she'd had to do. A decade ago she'd left Carter and married David Sutton, twenty years her senior, because Carter could never marry anyone either on paper or in fact. Because she'd loved Carter with a painful awareness of the necessary limitations of his commitment. Because Carter had cared for her too much to lie to her. And so she'd taken herself out of competition. She'd escaped in the traditional woman's way. Marriage to another. She hadn't seen Carter since.

"You're even more beautiful than I remembered," he told her.

She sat on a sofa, crossed her ankles, and slipped them neatly back under her. Her legs had the long, graceful curves of a model's.

"Homer will bring breakfast, too. Only toast and jam, I expect. The chef doesn't like to take time out from creating tonight's feast. I hope you understand."

She hoped he understood that he'd been invited up to visit, for nothing more, and that if he'd called at a more reasonable time they would have had their visit downstairs at one of the best tables or, if too crowded, then up there at the coffee table with the Grecian screen pulled across to hide her waiting bed.

"I understand," he said.

"Did David send you? Homer said you came about David."

"David's dead, Andrea. I'm sorry," he said kindly. He

didn't know any other way than the directness she herself
practiced. In the long run, it was kinder. No false hopes. "He
died in Budapest."

Her face went ashen with shock. Her gaze wandered
around the room as if looking for something to fasten onto, an
anchor, an explanation.

"You're sure?" she said at last.

"I was with him."

Two silent tears ran down her face. She looked up at
Carter.

"Please sit down," she said. "I'd like to know what
happened."

FOUR

In the flat above her exclusive Greek restaurant in Soho, Lady Andrea Sutton sat quietly on the sofa, hands folded in her lap, and listened without speaking as Nick Carter talked. After the news he'd brought her, he needed to lead up slowly to the questions he wanted answered.

Homer arrived with breakfast and left it covered on the coffee table as Carter described the meeting on Gellért Hill, the killing of Carol Romanescu, the drive through Budapest to the old hotel in Pest, and finally Sir David's heart attack.

"I'm sorry," he said when he'd finished. "He was a fine man to work with."

"We had some good times, didn't we."

She lifted covers from the plates on the tray on the coffee table before her. The delicious aromas of coffee, tea, toast, muffins, fruit jams, and marmalade mixed with the hot smell of the fire.

"I hope you're hungry," she said and poured him coffee.

She was putting off the inevitable—talking about her husband of ten years. Talking of what he'd meant and not meant to her, and whether he had loved her . . . and she him. Her movements were slow and deliberate, as if she were outside

35

herself, observing a shell of herself perform the little niceties of life.

"Actually," Carter said, "I'm starved."

He took the coffee and drank as she spread strawberry jam on a slice of toast. She laid the toast on a bone china plate and handed it to him.

"What about yourself?" he said.

She looked at the simple food on the tray, then up at him with wide gray eyes.

"Have some tea," he suggested.

"Yes. Of course."

She poured milk in a cup, laid the silver strainer over it, and tipped the teapot until the cup was full. She covered the teapot with a quilted cozy and put the strainer on a plate to drip. She poured in a spoonful of sugar, picked up the cup, and drank.

"Do you remember that time in Cairo?" he said.

She looked up over the cup.

"David in the bar," he went on. "What was it called?"

"The Nubian Oar."

"That's it." He smiled at her. "The Nubian Oar. And the veil dancer. She danced for David—came right up to him and started dropping her veils. You were laughing. Such a funny expression he had on his face. Not greed or lust at all. More like a five-year-old with a full cookie jar and a nanny lurking in the corner."

"And you were in the back room," she said. "Waiting."

"When the last veil came down, you both jumped under the table."

"And poison darts shot out from her hips. Would've killed us both. David yanked her down by the ankles while you shot her boss across the room."

"That's right," he said. "All hell broke loose. Saboteurs,

informers, police. You got the microdot from her navel while David and I were occupied.''

"They shot you in the arm. David was limping from a knife wound to the thigh.'' Her face was animated, almost rosy with the past, her voice breathless. "Somehow we got away.''

"Naguib was waiting on the Nile with the motorboat,'' he said, smiling. "It was a long mission, three months. A lot can happen in three months,'' he said quietly.

She closed her eyes, sipped tea.

"A lot,'' she murmured.

Carter ate the toast, drained the coffee, ate muffins and more toast, while she cradled her cup and occasionally drank. The room had a warm southern exposure, the small-paned windows shiny clean, the sky bright and Wedgwood blue above the smog line. Wrens hopped along the ledge. In the fireplace, the flames crackled.

"I loved him in a rather nice way,'' she said at last. "He didn't mind that it wasn't a consuming passion.'' She set down her cup. "He said he'd had enough of that to last a lifetime.'' She hesitated, her hand poised in front of her, her face taut with emotion. "We did things together . . . he was decent . . . very dear . . . to me . . .'' Tears spread down her cheeks. "No, no.'' She waved Carter away.

Still, he sat beside her and pulled her close. She gave in to weep helplessly into his shoulder. She shuddered with sobs. He handed her tissues, and she blew her nose and cried again.

He stroked her hair as she wept. He remembered their times together, the softness of her flesh, the insistence of her demands, the triumph in her cries afterward. The exhaustion of the last few days fell from him. Just her presence refreshed him. But he had a mission to do for Hawk, and that came first.

"He . . . asked you to tell me yourself, didn't he," she said, snuffling into a tissue. "If you were there, he'd want you to be the one."

"You and he must have been very close to have known what he'd want."

"He had ideals. Principles. David was special, admirable, in his own right."

"But he wasn't with MI5 any longer."

"Not that I know of."

She sighed, her head resting on his shoulder, warm against his throat. She smelled of tea roses.

"MI5 says he wasn't working for them," he said.

"Oh?"

"Then why did he kill Romanescu?"

"David didn't tell me everything."

"There was more?"

He drew back and looked questioningly into the soft gray eyes. He took the damp tissue from her hand, wiped the tear-streaked face, patted the eyes, then held it to her nose.

"Blow," he ordered.

Obediently, she blew into the tissue.

Tenderness welled inside him. He kissed her.

She gave a little gasp, went rigid.

He moved away.

"Another cup of tea," he said, "while you tell me what David had been doing with his time."

Following her ritual, he poured tea and then coffee for himself.

She watched him, the soft eyes disturbed, puzzled by a new inner turmoil. Or an old turmoil insistent on recognition.

"I assume even a busy restaurant wasn't enough to occupy David's inquisitive mind," he prompted.

"The restaurant's mine," she said simply. "I needed something to do after . . . after . . ."

"After you left the service."

She nodded, but the answer was incomplete. After she left the service, yes, but also after her affair with Carter. She'd needed a bridge back to ordinary life.

"David came and went," she said. "He helped with the accounts here. Sometimes he went up to our place in Cumbria—it was his place, really."

"Isolated and rugged there."

"Peaceful was the way David put it. Only nature to contend with."

She pushed herself from the sofa and stood up, a high-class, high-strung filly with a case of nerves. She strode to the window, twisting her fingers. She peeled the drape back to the casing, and sunlight streamed through the almost translucent fabric of her robe. Her curves were outlined sharp and inviting in a haze of glistening blue. She turned slowly, her nipples stiff silhouetted points. Unaware, she studied him as she continued.

"I don't know exactly what he did with his time. Cricket matches occasionally, Lord's or the Oval. When he was restless, he'd drink at the club. During the day we'd tour antique shops for pieces to take to the house in Cumbria. When I could get away we'd go to the theater, see friends, all the normal things people do."

"Did he talk about going back to work?"

"The service? I'm not sure. He was ambivalent when they discharged him. Part of him was angry and depressed. He was too young, still had too much he wanted to do. He'd look around and see misery and greed and mismanagement of evil proportions. It made him feel crazy sometimes, I think, to see so much wrong going unchanged."

"We all despise that."

"We do," she agreed. She let the drape fall from her hand. Her negligee swayed. "That's what attracts us to the work in the first place, those of us who do it for a reason other than thrills, money, or some stupid idea of glamorous adventure.''

She walked back across the room. She glanced at the bed, averted her eyes, then sat on the other sofa across from Carter.

"You said he was ambivalent," he said.

"The other part of him wanted to quit."

She leaned forward, elbows on knees, intense in her explanation. But she also leaned because she wanted to be closer to Carter, only the flimsy security of a coffee table a buffer against her growing recognition that she still wanted him, that out of pain came human need. She dipped her head, then looked up, eyes glowing, unknowingly calling him. He felt her power pulling, pulling. . . .

"He was tired of it all," she continued, "tired of the wounds and exhaustion and never, never being able to do enough. So many problems, so few solutions. And I think he didn't like the changes he saw in courts around the world. He didn't like the ease with which criminals seemed to be getting off. It made the job seem pointless. Why should he care so much that he constantly put his life on the line when the vast majority of the earth's citizens were allowing their legal systems to free lawbreakers, rapists, and murderers?"

"He asked questions that all of us ask."

"Then you see," she said, smiling, the gray eyes probing his face for answers to questions she didn't want to ask. Denial was easier than the truth. "He was a practical man, an ethical man, yet what could he do?"

"Kill Carol Romanescu."

"Quite. The head of the Romanian secret police and member of the Politburo. A powerful man, evil, his job was to *be* evil."

"A man with a wife and four children. For all David knew,

he might have been working for us. A mole. Ultrasecret. In any case, the killing was unauthorized. Murder.''

''But Romanescu! Look how treacherous he was! Torture, killing!''

''Are you telling me that to get him David turned rogue? A vigilante?''

She sighed, exasperated.

''Nick. I've told you everything I can think of to help. How could I have known exactly what was in David's mind? You say you saw him kill Romanescu. I don't question *you*. But how do I know you're telling me the truth? How do I know you haven't turned yourself, gone over? Maybe you killed Romanescu *and* David.''

She stood up, trembling with thoughts . . . torn, fighting growing rage at death, the unknown, and where her unruly, shocked needs were driving her.

He arose, stood next to her, and casually took out his cigarette case. The smell of tea roses on her alabaster skin swelled in his head. He remembered the sight and feel of her hot, smooth thighs as he came down between them. His hands trembled, and he was sharply aware of that deep recess where all men store the primitive maleness that even civilization can't completely erase. He wanted her. Now.

He forced himself to light a cigarette.

''Or, maybe, David's still alive.'' She clenched her hands. ''Maybe this is all a trick! A nightmare! Maybe the KGB's sent you to kill me, too!''

She lunged, weeping, and beat her fists against his chest.

He put out his cigarette.

''What have you done with David?'' she cried.

He held her shoulders, shaking her, as she bruised his flesh.

''Andrea! Stop it!''

''I hate you! Hate you!''

He grabbed her fists and crushed them in a tight knot against him.

She spat in his face.

He slapped hers.

Shocked, they stared naked truth into one another's eyes. The years evaporated. He picked her up.

"Nick!"

She moaned and wrapped her arms around his neck. She kissed his throat, cheek, ear.

Desire shot urgent and demanding through his veins. Carrying her, he hurried across the room toward the bed.

She tore at his necktie. He stood her on the bed, ran his hands up over the svelte curves, capturing the breasts, the nipples. His thumbs on the nipples.

She gasped.

He ripped the flimsy robe as he pulled it open. Her breasts swung. Beneath, the alabaster skin converged on the triangle of warm brown female hair.

She glanced down at herself, surprised. She looked up. Her eyes blazed into his. He caught his breath. She pulled at his belt, zipper, pants, and he watched her, his breathing ragged, until at last the room's chill air struck his belly and legs.

He caught her, threw her down onto the bed, he moved once more between those smooth, hot legs. They rocked together, concentrating as if the world had stopped for them, until the explosions began and their shouts filled the room and the universe.

FIVE

Droning motors, punctuated occasionally by horns and shouts, seemed distant as if from another planet rather than being just below the Soho apartment above the Greek restaurant. The big bedroom was quiet, filled with thoughts and the heady smell of good sex.

Andrea Sutton curled over and around Nick Carter, her skin warm and damp, her fingers spread now in open acceptance . . . and ownership . . . on his chest. Guile and lies were gone, destroyed by the reality of the past.

"I suppose somewhere I knew," she murmured, almost to herself.

"Knew?"

"Knew that I still wanted you."

He smiled.

"I never stopped wanting you," he said.

"You never started," she retorted.

"Oh, that."

She laughed, a small laugh on herself tinged with the bitterness of self-betrayal.

"*That*," she agreed. "You never told me otherwise. You're too honest, or is there such a thing as being too honest? There were times when I would've liked you to lie even a little, say that we'd live together forever and ever, make a life suited to both of us, commitment, 'til death do us part.''

He pressed her tightly to him, a sharp pain of regret piercing his heart.

''I'm sorry,'' he said. ''The way I live . . . I've already made a commitment, but it's to my work.''

''You're married to your work.''

''I don't want a divorce.''

She leaned back, smiling at him with understanding.

''Once I thought I could never leave the service either,'' she said. ''It's funny, now that I remember. Of course I could leave. I did. And you could too. It has nothing to do with what one can and can't do. That's the lie we tell ourselves. We make choices, and your choice was to stay. Andrea vs. AXE. You chose AXE.'' There was no recrimination in her voice, only disappointment in herself for not being more desirable, more persuasive, more . . . necessary.

''Maybe I didn't have a choice,'' he said thoughtfully as he stroked her cheek. ''We're the summation of our experiences, or so psychologists tell us, and how they've affected our basic genetic material. Maybe my account totals Killmaster, no options, just as yours totals flexibility, several options. Neither of us is more right or wrong. It's just the way we are, and there was nothing you could have done, nothing more you could have been, nothing—absolutely nothing—that would have made it possible for me to live my life differently, unless I were to allow my living to become meaningless.''

''The premier Killmaster. The best. No exceptions.''

''I don't think about it that way.''

''If you did, you couldn't do it. You'd be distracted from devoting yourself to it.''

He smiled now, caught in her earnestness.

"Don't respect me too much," he said. "It doesn't become you. You were damned good yourself."

"That was a long time ago."

She sighed, and the perfume of her tea rose scent seemed to swirl in the air with her warm breath. He looked at her face, seeing the fine cobwebbing of age lines at the sides of her eyes and across her forehead. Once again tenderness mixed with desire welled inside him.

"I remember clearly how good you were," he told her. "An excellent agent."

She smiled, her gray eyes alight. She kissed him, and the playful kiss turned serious with intent. Her lips grew hot, yielding. He crushed her to him, wanting to draw her inside where she'd never hurt again, where he'd have her forever.

Her tongue darted between his lips, explored his teeth, the roof of his mouth. He bent her head back, trailing his lips along her jawline to her ear. She dug her fingers into his shoulders and moaned. His heart beat into his head, throbbing energy, need.

They rolled across the bed, feinting, playing, panting, until he captured her and she greedily spread her legs open to receive him.

"Look how high the sun is," she remarked, gazing from the bed across to the small-paned windows. "The morning must be half gone."

Her rich brown hair lay in damp ringlets around her face. He touched a curl, felt the hair smooth and slick.

"Do you have to go?" he said.

"Yes. But I won't."

She sat up abruptly and threw the blankets from the bed. And as goose bumps rose on his skin from the chill London air, she kissed him from neck to toes and back again, joyous laughter bubbling between them.

"Enough!" he cried at last.

"Torture?" she said and pulled the covers tight over them.

"The kind I like," he said, smiling at the woman who had once almost stolen his heart with her own devotion to duty . . . and to him. But love wasn't enough.

She shivered.

"To think David is dead," she murmured wonderingly. "I shall miss him. Such a cheerful chap. We had good years." She rested her head on his shoulder, and he wrapped his arms around her. "He would have understood this." She nodded as if to include the bed and all that had gone before in the last few hours. "An affirmation of life somehow."

"He would want you to go on. Find new happinesses."

"I suppose he would," she said slowly.

"And David's legacy," he said. "It's time to talk about that."

"Legacy? What legacy?"

"What had he done since he left the service?"

"I told you. As far as I can tell, nothing significant." A small hint of hurt, perhaps suspicion, crept into her voice.

"It would be David's legacy," he soothed her. "David wouldn't leave the world without willing something of himself, something he cared about, to go on after him."

She looked at him, now openly suspicious.

"David couldn't have changed all that much in ten years," he pressed. "It would be useless to try to convince me he had."

She was silent, studying him and his words with confusion.

"I wouldn't even know where to look," she said at last. She closed her eyes and sank back against his arm. "If it's a legacy, he'd have written it down. I don't know anything about special wills to the world. We each had regular wills, of course, but they deal only with money and property. I inherit

all his, just as he would've inherited mine.
except for David's from that earlier marriage. The boy w
a baronet now. Imagine that. Sir Kern Sutton, but he has a
trust . . .''

As she talked on in her quiet voice, Carter's mind traveled
back through the years. With her in his arms, ten years ago
was yesterday, and he remembered clearly the vibrant,
idealistic David. Saw him sitting at hotel desks, in train and
jet seats, on waiting room benches, and in office chairs, with
a notebook before him and a fountain pen in his hand.

"Haiku!" Carter said.

"What?" she said, startled from her reverie.

"Haiku. Unrhymed Japanese verse. Where are his
notebooks?''

She knew instantly what he meant, but she hesitated.

"I don't know," she said slowly. "They're probably
personal . . . intimate. . . . I don't think he'd have wanted
anyone to see them . . .''

"Of course they are. But we're not interested in that, only
in what they can tell us about Romanescu and what else
David might have been doing. Maybe he never told you. He
used to hide in his poetry anything he had to keep but didn't
want found. It was a reliable, secret method. He could have
still been using it.''

She closed her eyes, worry momentarily crossing her face.
She seemed to steel herself. She opened her eyes.

"Very well. Come along.''

She started to pull away.

"Wait,'' he said. He drew her back and looked solemnly at
her. "Not that way.'' He kissed her, holding her tense
resistance against his warmth. "I care about you. It's not just
my work.'' His lips searched her shoulder, throat, the hollow
between her breasts, and she sighed, the muscles relaxing.
"You were very important to me. You still are.''

ere was laughter in her voice.
laughing at herself.

'll do it to myself again,'' she said.

. If I stay here any longer I'll convince
ve with you. Get up. We'll find David's

picked up the blue negligee from the floor,
holding up to admire the long rip. She laughed again,
breasts bouncing, and tossed it toward a wicker wastebasket.
It landed in a cloud of pale blue on the floor.

"I'll buy you another," he said as he dropped it into the
wastebasket and picked up his pants. "Something that will
drive me really mad next time."

They both laughed, prolonging the closeness of the
lovemaking, as they showered and dressed, always watching
one another. He once again put on the Bonn suit, and she
dressed in camel-colored slacks and a café-au-lait sweater
that made her rich brown hair glint with new, inviting life full
of promise.

There were three notebooks, simple, thick, spiral notebooks
that any child would carry to school. None was dated, the
handwriting the same in all three. Two were filled with verses
and notes for verses, and one contained mentions of the
Nubian Oar bar in Cairo. Quickly Carter discarded those two
books.

The third notebook's pages were also crammed with jot-
tings, but the last quarter of it was empty. Carter started from
the back.

> *Storm and hail for good*
> *do rain on Pest's Eger U., or*
> *life does come from death.*

And before that was:

> *Repair and damage,*
> *persistent attempts at change*
> *the mechanic loses.*

The garage on the Eger U. in Pest came instantly to Carter's mind. A short, one-block-long street with only one garage for repairing automobiles—and hiding those being followed.

"What does it mean?" Andrea said, puzzled.

"I don't know yet."

Carter read silently to himself the third poem:

> *Stars, infinity*
> *remorseless mortality*
> *evolves on Gellért.*

The first mention of Romanescu—killed by David on Gellért Hill.

"Well," she said, "as much as I loved and respected him, I must say he was a terrible poet."

"Do you mind if I take this notebook?"

"Actually, I do mind. If it's his, I want it. At least for a while, until I have time to make some decisions." She looked at him, and smiled a smile that asked his understanding.

"You'll want to read through it yourself," he said. "No doubt he talks about you, his feelings for you."

"If he does . . . I suppose it's silly now that he's dead . . . but I would like to know."

"Of course." He carried the notebook to an upright desk and took out his pen. "I'll copy what I need. Watch, if you like."

"I'll watch you," she said. "Just you."

They walked down the fragile circular staircase. It was a little past noon, and the air was filled with the spicy Greek smells of *dolmades*, minced meat and rice rolled up in cabbage leaves, *souvlakia*, vegetables and meats roasted on a spit, and *moussaka*, a casserole of eggplant, ground lamb, and white sauce. Talk, laughter, and Greek folk music filtered through the door at the bottom of the staircase.

On the bottom step she stopped and looked back up at him.

"I forgot," she said, worried. "Oh, well. Nothing to be done. You'll just have to meet them."

"Who? What?"

"Come along and be a good chap."

She opened the door and the full range of the restaurant's aromas and sounds intensified to party level. Suddenly he knew what she was talking about.

"I thought you were closed for lunch," he said.

"We have special clubs we allow to have lunches here occasionally. It brings new customers to the dinner business."

They retraced his steps through the restaurant, empty except for a single, long table in the middle of the largest room. The other tables had been pushed back against the walls so the long central table with the men—Carter counted eleven—talking, laughing, drinking retsina and aretsinoto wines, and eating Greek food, could be served properly. Three waiters hovered near the door to the kitchen. The restaurant prided itself on food and service.

"Andrea!" the patrons called out, welcoming her while glancing curiously behind her at Carter.

As she and Carter moved past the table, the men congratulated her on the excellent food and wine, the ambience, and her personal beauty. She handled the compliments graciously, until one asked about David.

She stopped, stared, and at last answered.

"He's dead, I'm afraid."

Stunned silence filled the room. A waiter at the door wheeled and ran into the clattering kitchen. Instantly there was silence from there, too.

Carter recognized faces in the exclusive club. Mr. Justice Paul Stone. Cabinet minister Bertie Allen. William Reid, M.P. Lord Nathan Fackler, owner of Brookland Motors. Others less familiar, but important, and some distinguished.

"What happened?" Justice Stone asked for all of them.

"He died in Budapest. His heart at last." She didn't look at them. "Our friend Nick just brought me the news."

"Budapest?" echoed one. "What was he doing in Budapest? I thought he'd gone to Cumbria."

"Probably some secret action of the P.M.'s," said another. "What about it, Bertie? Know anything?"

Bertie Allen shook his gray head.

"Not a bloody thing," he said. "Doubt it'd filter down from Ten Downing, you know."

"We'll have a memorial service for the old boy," Justice Stone said. "Would that be all right, Andrea? The club organizing a service?"

"Thank you, Paul," Andrea murmured. "Anything you'd like. I'm sure David would have felt honored."

She took Carter's arm, and he knew she wanted to leave, didn't want to face more questions, more sympathetic looks, more compassion. In the beginning, sympathy was a burden.

"I have a plane to catch," Carter told the men. They'd already broken into clusters to discuss David Sutton's death and the most appropriate memorial. "Andrea?"

Grateful, she escorted him out into the hall and then into the foyer.

"Sorry," she breathed.

"There was no way around them."

"I'll wait out here a bit until they settle down. Maybe I can sneak past later."

He held her chin and looked at her. She smiled wanly.

"I'll miss you," he said.

"But not enough."

"Sorry."

"No need to be. I'm grown up. Where do you go next?"

"Heathrow."

"Then you are flying on." She bit her lower lip. "Will I see you again?"

"Of course." He smiled. "I owe you a nightgown."

SIX

Like a lady in a white lace dress, Paris seemed always on the verge of a party. With its rococo architecture, frilly trees, vast gardens, wide boulevards, and inviting sidewalk cafés and flower vendors, the three million residents of the City of Lights put up with sky-high rents, poor telephone connections, and abominable traffic snarls because *ce soir*—tonight—or certainly *demain*—tomorrow—all dreams of love and laughter would be fulfilled.

As Nick Carter strode toward the next address in David Sutton's haiku lines, he considered the Parisians bustling around him. The men, cigarettes dangling from the corners of their mouths, hands dug deep into pockets, eyed the women. The women, with haughty heads held high, watched the men through eyelashes thickened with mascara. Old and young, they carried an air of irresistible cynicism and hope. In Paris, even for those who knew better, all things were possible.

It made Carter smile. Soon, they seemed to be saying, fine wines from Burgundy would flow in a river as endless as the Seine. Students at the Sorbonne would abandon their books for a hands-on study of life. Painters and writers would leave their Montmartre attics to gather at Les Deux Magots on the Boulevard St.-Germain to honor the ghosts of Picasso,

Hemingway, and Sartre. Businessmen and plumbers, car builders and beauticians, international bankers and whores would rally in a convulsion of theatrical fun as honest as any of the other lies told about romantic Paris and its promise of never-ending happiness.

Carter was one of them. With his narrow tie, wide-collared artist's shirt, and threadbare brown suit he strode along the Rue de Jardin, smiling, enjoying the exuberant energy around him. It gave added spring to his step, and hope of success for this difficult, puzzling mission.

On the flight from London, he'd memorized the haikus from David Sutton's notebook, and then destroyed his copies. His memory was as reliable, and certainly much more secure.

Now he was almost at what he hoped was the correct destination hidden in the next haiku:

> *Fashion clicks its heels*
> *as 23 models prance*
> *through Paris's garden street.*

Above the black enameled door at 23 Rue de Jardin—Garden Street—the dignified, gold-leafed sign—Emmanuel St. Croix—told Carter he was right. In the single window, a plastic mannequin with arched brows stood in perpetual readiness, a hand extended, as she displayed a flowing black silk and tulle evening gown.

Carter opened the door.

"Please come in and rest," a female voice said immediately in French. "Monsieur and madame are out, but they will return soon."

A long sofa and clusters of chairs ran along the perimeter of the simple white room. Inexpensive but elegant tables, lamps, and ashtrays waited for prospective, dress-buying customers. Emmanuel St. Croix was a small, select house of fashionable eveningwear, and everyone but the store's mechanical greeting service was out.

Carter walked across the empty room, past other mannequins modeling more gowns, to a door at the back. He opened it onto piles of colorful fabrics and trims, half-clothed dressers' dummies, and a long table with scissors, threads, pattern papers, and pins. Again, no people. Instantly the mechanical recording spoke.

"Please return to the foyer," it said sternly. "Our automatic guard systems will ring if you try to carry out any of our creations."

Carter closed the door. Quickly, efficiently, he searched the room, beneath the bolts of cloth, behind boxes of trim and accessories, among flats of samples. He went through the area thoroughly, paying attention to even the smallest needles. Nothing. It was just what it looked like on the surface—a working design room.

He opened the door again.

"Please return to the foyer," the voice repeated sternly, obviously triggered by a toggle on the door hinge. "Our automatic guard systems will ring if you try to carry out any of our creations."

Carter searched the white waiting room, but again he found nothing unusual. With a sweep of his gaze, he took it in one last time—the stark walls, the simple, elegant furniture—then he opened the front door.

"Please come in and rest," the woman's voice invited again. "Monsieur and madame are out, but they will return soon."

He closed the door grimly and once more joined the potential on Rue de Jardin.

The fashion world was as untrusting as ever. But now instead of thin-lipped, undernourished women and musclebound homosexuals to guard the design secrets, modern technology was in charge.

Why had David Sutton described the Emmanuel St. Croix shop? A joke, perhaps? David had liked his jokes. Or . . . had someone warned them Carter was coming?

Making the transatlantic call was actually faster and less trouble than phoning from Paris's Left to Right Bank. Even in a rich metropolis, life was a series of priorities.

When Carter made the connection, it was 10 A.M. in Washington, and the busyness of the day sounded in Hawk's brusque greeting. Carter made his report.

"So that garage in Budapest was described in Sutton's haiku," Hawk said thoughtfully and expelled a noisy gust of cigar smoke. "But you found nothing at the Rue de Jardin address. Could be a decoy. Could be a drop. Could be just about anything."

"Or nothing."

"Hmmm."

Carter listened to the distant, absentminded puffing. The AXE chief's computerlike mind was digesting Carter's information, sorting and filing it, then matching it with information from other agents.

"I don't like it," Hawk said at last. "Damn. No way to tell whether there's a connection to the assassinations here. And we're still working to find any other lead. Checking other terrorist groups. Fanatical organizations. So far, no one's stepped forward to claim responsibility. Everything's too quiet. The calm before a bloodletting. They're well organized, smart, and informed. To pull off those synchronized attacks, they had to be. Their potential is appalling."

"Perhaps losing five of their people in the Washington assassination attempts slowed them down."

"Perhaps." Hawk sounded doubtful. "I want real

answers. No more speculation. I trust you're off to check out
the next haiku clue?''

"The Netherlands, sir."

"Make it fast, N3. Very fast."

Vibrant red, yellow, pink, orange, and ivory tulips spread in
row after row of color across the rich North Sea countryside.
The early spring air was chill, the sharp smell of sea salt a
pleasant reminder of the expanse of ocean over the horizon.

Like most of the Dutch in the coastal bulb-growing region
north and south of Haarlem, Carter pedaled a fat-tired bike on
the dirt road, passing parents with children in bike carriers
cradling arms full of tulips to present to their schoolteachers.

Despite increased mechanization and the billion-dollar
growth of agribusiness, Holland's bulb growing was still
primarily a small, family-operated industry. More than
eighty percent of the farms in the area were a dozen acres or
less, and each family member pitched in for spring flower
tending and cutting, summer harvesting, and autumn plant-
ing.

Carter watched the beauty of the countryside and felt the
welcome sweat of pedaling a long distance on the flat land.
Here and there workers were out, surveying the flowers,
some already cutting off blooms to force the plants' energies
into the bulbs.

He pedaled on, seeing fewer and fewer people. At last his
destination appeared off in the distance.

The farm was fifteen miles off the main highway, a cluster
of neat whitewashed buildings at the end of a straight road. It
would be an ideal hideout. An ordinary farm like any other,
and in an excellent location for identifying intruders—flat
land covered with low flowers. Anything taller than three feet
stood out like a skyscraper.

He pedaled slowly now, as if having trouble. He twisted

the front wheel back and forth, fighting a nonexistent flat.

He shook his head, disgusted, and jumped off the bike in the shade of one of the few trees. He took a handkerchief from his back pocket, wiped his face, and gazed in irritation around him as if by simply demanding it, help would arrive.

Of course, no one did, and he was pleased. But he kicked the bike and slumped against the tree trunk. He looked ahead. The land was empty of people, and the farm's buildings were clustered so tightly together that he couldn't see anyone there. But that didn't mean that they couldn't see him.

Impatient again, he looked around, scratched his head, then studied the tall tree. He would climb it and watch for help.

He jumped, hooked a hand over a branch, and with a brief intake of breath pulled himself up into the thick leaves. Once stabilized on a branch, he reached inside his jacket and took out collapsible, powerful binoculars. For a moment he savored the security of the feel of his Luger in the small of his back, then he adjusted the binoculars.

The farm came into focus, and he smiled a cold smile full of knowledge. At last he'd found something worthwhile.

There were seven buildings. A farmhouse, a barn, and five smaller buildings. The five smaller buildings appeared to be three-walled shelters with roofs. The walls facing the courtyards were open. And in the center of the courtyard—he adjusted his binoculars to be sure—two men were practicing maneuvers with small submachine guns. Ingrams. They feinted, aimed, and shot at dummies swinging like dead men from poles in the yard. The open buildings were obviously sound absorbers. He could see only the results of the bullets' impact—the wildly dancing dummies. The sounds were distant snaps, like the snap of a dry tree branch. Not particularly noticeable in a land of wind and birds.

He watched the men long enough to determine that they

weren't self-taught. They were good. Professionally trained. And they hadn't learned their skills for road shows or exhibitions. They knew how to kill, and they thrilled to it.

He replaced the binoculars under his shirt and jumped down from the tree. It was time to go after more information.

He worked beside his bike, taking off the tire, patching the imaginary hole, then putting the tire back on. At last, wiping his face and hands on his handkerchief, he resumed the bicycle ride that would apparently, innocently, take him beyond the farm.

He pedaled past a green field in which black and white cows feasted on a mound of tulip blossoms cut and donated by their bulb-growing owner, while on the other side of the road, rows and rows of spectacular red tulips jauntily waved their crimson heads. After four hundred years of Dutch bulb culture, the farmers knew precisely when to plant, cut, and harvest the hybrids and descendants of the species brought originally from the mountainsides of central Asia.

As he rode across the bridge over a low canal, he glanced expertly around but saw no one.

He pitched off the bicycle.

Dragged it into the ditch.

Crawled along the sloping banks toward the farm buildings.

Birds sang, cows lowed, and multihued tulips stretched far into the distance. The air was dank with the smell of mud and water. Counting steps, he topped the canal bank close to the farm.

He took out his Luger, balanced it, and dashed over the open, grassy land.

Stopped. Pressed close to the back of the barn. He heard only the songs of birds and the soft rustle of the wind. No cracks from the acoustically muffled Ingrams. No talking. No running. Nothing.

He slipped toward the edge of the whitewashed building. Peered around it at the courtyard. He saw no one.

Pressed flat against the building, his extraordinary senses ready to react to any sight or sound, the Luger aimed in front of him, he moved quickly toward the yard.

Now with the whole yard in view from his post at the barn's corner, he saw that no one was there. One dummy still swayed, its body riddled with holes. The men and the Ingrams had gone.

Either someone had seen him, or they'd been warned by an undetectable electronic system. In either case, they'd be after him.

Splinters burst into his face, the bullet lodged three inches from his ear.

Instantly he ducked, firing in return at a moving shadow that darted behind one of the acoustical sheds.

He pursued, slipping along the barn, dashing toward the shed.

A bullet bit into the dirt at his feet.

He crouched and fired at a lanky man with a patch over one eye.

The man sped away, a .45 automatic in his hand. He'd been one of the men with the Ingrams, but the submachine guns were meant for other kinds of battles. If there was only one opponent, a .45 was fairer. They were killers, but their pride gave them their own set of ethics.

He fired again as the man with the patch disappeared behind another shed. Had he imagined it, or had the man suddenly lost his balance as if hit in the leg?

He raced after, the hairs on the back of his neck rising. He was being watched.

Suddenly he spun on his heel.

Clicked his stiletto Hugo into his hand.

Hurled it across fifteen feet to lodge through another man's sleeve into the house's wall.

Pinned, the man yanked at his arm.

Carter tore across the distance.

The man saw him. Raised his .45, aimed.

Carter slashed it from his hand before he could shoot.

"Killmaster!" the man shouted in English as if in warning to someone else.

Carter grabbed the man's jacket and jerked him once. The arm came free. He was a small man with the knotted muscles of a weight lifter. But the muscles were excessive for the agility of close fighting. Still, he lifted his arms and easily broke Carter's hold with the snap of his forearms.

Carter didn't wait to argue. He bashed a fist into the weight lifter's jaw.

Astonished, the weight lifter stopped. He shook his head as if to clear it. But it was too late. His eyes rolled up into his head. Like a sack of potatoes, he collapsed against the house.

Carter picked up the stiletto and slipped it back into the chamois case on his forearm. He turned, alert for signs of the second man.

Carefully, listening, watching, he moved around to the front of the house that looked out on the courtyard.

There he saw it. A shadow that moved far across the yard, a slow movement of stealth. It seemed to compress into a ball.

Carter returned to the farmhouse's wall where the weight lifter still lay unconscious. He didn't even moan.

Carter glanced at him. Then, with the silence and speed of a predatory jungle cat, he raced around the perimeter of the seven buildings.

Even a Killmaster gets a break occasionally. The man with the eye patch squatted at the side of a shed, his gaze glued to the house where Carter had been. He was waiting for Carter to give him a target.

Blood from one of Carter's bullets spread in a pool on the man's pants leg. He was the compact shadow, and he hadn't moved since Carter had spotted him. He wasn't particularly bright, but he would have information. Carter allowed himself a short smile of anticipation. Information at last.

He stepped silently to the man's back and stuck his Luger in the man's ear.

"Let's talk," Carter said in English.

The man went rigid. He flung an arm around, trying to catch Carter off balance.

Carter kicked the arm. And in one smooth movement, he leaned over, shoved the man down on his back, and pressed the Luger to his aquiline nose. There was no way the man was going to try any more tricks. Carter sat on his chest and made himself comfortable.

"Let's talk," Carter repeated.

The eye that wasn't hidden behind a patch stared in fear. The man licked dry lips.

"Was?"

Carter repeated the order in German.

The man breathed heavily, trying to figure a way to resist.

"Now!" Carter said, pushing the Luger hard against the nose.

The face exploded. Blood, flesh, and cartilage sprayed into the air.

Carter hadn't fired. Someone else had killed the man. Someone with a long-distance, powerful rifle of high accuracy, aiming from the house.

The ground shook.

A fireball erupted where the house had been.

Carter jumped back.

The barn exploded, then the shed next to it. Wood, heat, and smoke filled the air.

Carter tore away from the area as the sheds blasted to bits one by one until only smoke, debris, and the stillness of death lay on the fertile Dutch plain.

The hideout was gone, and the men who had been its inhabitants were dead. Either the weight lifter Carter had knocked out next to the house had recovered long enough to push the switch, or a third person had done it. Like the captured assassin in Washington, D.C., who had killed himself, the men here had been willing martyrs to a cause.

Would-be martyrs were vicious adversaries. They had already promised their lives. Their deaths were the expected and desired fulfillment of their contracts. Carter needed to move immediately to the destination in the next haiku.

SEVEN

The house Nick Carter was looking for was on Hamburg's Schäferkampsallee, not far from the Jewish community center. He parked the small Mercedes 180 he'd rented in Haarlem, took out his briefcase, and walked down the street.

In the short noontime shadows of the bright spring sunshine, young Jewish boys in skullcaps played kickball along an alley while their sisters watched, giggling modestly behind their hands. Across the street, four men with prayer shawls sat on a porch, talking Talmud and drinking glasses of tea brought by a quiet woman whose hair was hidden beneath the traditional dark scarf.

As Carter strolled along the street, he remembered that in 1933 there were twenty-five thousand Jews living in Hamburg. About half of them emigrated as the Nazis rose to power. The rest were sent to concentration camps. Most died there. Now, less than two thousand Jews lived in Hamburg, a mixed lot, mostly refugees from Eastern Europe, but they lived with a peace and freedom unimaginable in Germany before the Nazi horror.

Carter swung his briefcase, a prosperous realtor or insurance broker, a skullcap snug to his head as if it belonged there, and strode up the front walk of the modest house whose

64

address had been in David Sutton's next haiku.

The four men across the street briefly studied Carter, then returned with vigor to their Talmudic argument. They would have been teen-agers when they were sent to Auschwitz or Bergen-Belsen. They had survived and raised families of their own, scarred and strengthened by their unasked-for heritage. The human soul was limitless.

As Carter walked, he took out a set of skeleton keys, holding them tight in his hand where they couldn't be seen. The house appeared deserted. He knocked at the door. When no one answered, he tested the keys until the right one at last turned.

He glanced once over his shoulder before he opened the door. The kickball game continued in the alleyway. The discussion reached new animation on the porch. He opened the door and went in.

The house had been stripped bare. He walked through the empty rooms. Only the faint, stale odor of old cigarettes remained. It was a small house, well tended. No dust, dirt, or trash had been left to ruin the welcome of the next inhabitants—or to inform the curious of who had lived there and where they'd gone.

They'd done a thorough job. Still, Carter checked floors, walls, ceilings, windowsills, wall vents, electrical outlets, furnace, medicine cabinet, kitchen cupboards. He found nothing.

He walked slowly through the rooms, thinking, imagining himself living in the two-bedroom house, rising in the morning, eating, working . . . all the little usual acts that in the end, by their habitual ordinariness, give character to a life and, to the keen observer, tell more than a person might wish.

He smiled wryly. Of course.

He walked back into the kitchen, to the hole in the wall where a phone had been connected.

He found the spot his eyes had passed over and dismissed twenty minutes ago. Only with thinking did it become important.

It was a tiny spot next to where the telephone had been. There a steel wool pad had scrubbed the wall's shiny paint into dullness. Someone had talked on the phone and written a note to himself on the wall, then erased it.

Carter opened the briefcase and took out a narrow bottle. Using the brush attached to the cap, he dotted on the special AXE chemical. Slowly a word appeared, faint but readable: Lübeck. He worked on the next line. Too much chemical, and the writing would disappear altogether. Too little, and it would remain illegible.

At last, numbers and letters began to appear. It was an address.

The birthplace of Thomas Mann and the legendary setting of his first novel, *Buddenbrooks*, Lübeck is a shirt-sleeves-and-muscle city of more than two hundred thousand people. Downtown architectural monuments housing modern industry, busy docks on the Baltic Sea, and hilly forests and meadows yielding rich resources testify to the hearty, beer-saluting, hard-working laborers, artisans, and businessmen who made Lübeck another of modern West Germany's contributions to practical prosperity.

Carter drove north along the old streets, past the brick buildings dating from medieval times, toward the address on the outskirts of the former capital of the Hanseatic League. He was almost out of gas. The drive from Hamburg north to Lübeck had been only thirty miles, but then he'd been low when he'd left that afternoon.

He stopped at a gas station, asked the attendant to fill the tank, and walked toward the rest room.

And stopped. Stared at the headlines on the array of newspapers outside the office. He dropped a coin in a slot, picked up the *Berliner Zeitung*, and turned to an inside page of international news.

Quickly he read the short articles. Fanatical PLO leader Ali al-Assad had been murdered late yesterday in Damascus; Israeli guerrillas were suspected. Self-declared Emperor Jomuro Momonatumbo of Namibia, called the Baby-Killer by his people, had been assassinated in his vacation palace on the South Atlantic. A subsequent military coup had already replaced him with a colonel who was alleged to have five hundred wives.

Carter snapped the paper closed, folded it under his arm, and walked to a telephone booth.

"What do you have?" Hawk wasted no words as soon as he heard Carter's voice.

Carter described briefly the explosive deaths in Holland, the deserted house in Hamburg, and the address he'd at last found written there.

"Lübeck, eh?"

In far-off Washington, the AXE chief's butane lighter snapped, and he dragged noisily on a new cigar.

"It appears promising. No one could know I have it."

"Best lead we've had so far," Hawk said sourly. "Damn. It's not enough!"

"The assassins are exceptionally good," Carter agreed. "Careful, and willing to give their lives for their cause. Did you get anything on the Assad and Momonatumbo killings?"

"You saw that?" Hawk's voice allowed itself a note of pleasure in Carter's reliably quick intelligence. "Yes. Death warrants were left on both men. The same type as those we found here."

The two men were silent as they worried over the implications.

"More evidence of an international conspiracy," Carter said at last.

"Unfortunately true. We didn't learn about the new warrants until this morning. Both countries tried to keep them quiet. But our people are persistent."

"Anything about Romanescu's killing?"

"No one's claimed responsibility, if that's what you mean. And no death warrant has arrived in Bucharest. Neither the Hungarian or Romanian authorities have connected Sutton to it, and we see no point in informing them at this point."

"Sutton could have been investigating the conspiracy, or he could have been a member of it," Carter said thoughtfully.

"Exactly, N3. And it doesn't much matter right now with both men dead."

"The information is what counts."

"Where will they kill next?" Hawk said, his gravelly voice rising. "Who are they, and why? They missed twice here in the United States. They'll try again. Get to that address, N3. We must stop them!"

The old house rose stark and somber high above the Baltic. Carter caught glimpses of it through the forest of firs that blanketed the mountainside as he drove up the winding road.

It was a tall narrow house with a tower and sharply pitched roof. The white walls were weathered to the color of sun-bleached bones. The bottom half of the house and the walls around the windows were decorated with a crosshatching of dark, stained timbers.

As he drew closer, he could see the style was heavy fifteenth-century Hessian architecture, but that the more modern builder had added telephone wires, a television antenna, and a cement drive with striped posts to mark the way up the steep hill during a bad snowstorm.

Carter drove up with his window down, enjoying the cold crisp smells of wind and pine. The late afternoon shadows were long and black, wavering across the drive with the wind as it blew through the trees.

His briefcase and a dignified homburg were beside him on the front seat. The skullcap was gone. He still wore the expensive, tailored Bonn business suit. As he pulled to a stop beside a mud-spattered Jeep at the top of the house's drive, he felt his personality change subtly to help play the part of the new character he was already developing.

A Killmaster had not only skills in guns, knives, and bombs. He was also—and often more importantly—a master of deception. Information was easier to obtain from the living than it was from the dead.

Carter took out a small device from the briefcase and concealed it against his palm. He stepped out of the Mercedes, closed the door, and listened. The thrilling music of Beethoven's Fifth Symphony drifted from the Hessian house. He smiled, let the music swell in his head, a welcome respite but also . . . somehow . . . a warning. . . .

He walked toward the scrubbed front steps, and as he rang the bell, he noted the bright red spring geraniums on either side in raked planters, and the spectacular one-hundred-eighty-degree panorama of the green valley and glistening sea below. The house was not only costly and remote, its beauty was also carefully tended to.

"Ja?"

The man who opened the door was about sixty, pale, with the stooped, rounded shoulders of one who lived in books. He didn't look like an assassin. But he was alive . . . and unsuspecting. Carter smiled. Beethoven's symphony spread through the doorway and into the crisp air.

"Jan Marburg from Michelstadt," Carter announced himself in flawless German. He rotated the secret device against his palm and smiled a self-assured businessman's smile. "My father is an architect. He designed this house in 1952 for the Van Landaus. Our firm is buying up one or two prime examples from each period; and paying a damned good price, if I say so myself. It's Hessian, you see, like the architecture in Michelstadt—"

"Come back in the morning," the man said, peering up over half glasses. His watery blue eyes were distracted. "Come back in the morning." He had a fine-featured small face, thick curly white hair, and nervous hands that missed their accustomed book. At his sides, the fingers twitched and pulled at the woolly trousers. "Beethoven! Beethoven!"

He glanced back into the dark behind him as if to make certain the music he heard was indeed his, and Carter slipped the device against the door lock.

"Will you be here in the morning?" Carter wanted to know. "I can assure you, you won't be disappointed. The money is excellent."

The nervous hands moved into the air in front of the little man. He flicked them at Carter as if he were an annoying moth.

"Tomorrow!" he insisted, then stepped back and slammed the door.

Carter smiled, turned on his heel, and—the strains of the symphony's third movement sweet to his ears—strode to his car.

Once again down the drive and temporarily hidden from the house's view, Carter parked the Mercedes off the road in a stand of aromatic pine. He stripped off the businessman's suit and put on a black jump suit. He slipped his 9mm Luger

Wilhelmina into the holster under his shirt on his left side, restrapped his stiletto Hugo to his wrist, and adjusted Pierre, his gas bomb, on his inner thigh.

He moved silently away from the car and up the green mountainside. Birds sang. Insects chirruped. The sun hung orange and soft on the horizon.

He climbed on, aware of the sun, the direction of the road's switchbacks, the growing strains of Beethoven's Fifth, until at last the tall house loomed like a giant bird of prey directly above. He took out his Luger.

He angled to the right, coming in toward the house from the west on a brick walk. He paused at windows and saw rooms full of dark, heavy furniture but no people. He moved on until he reached the front door.

He pushed the handle. The door swung quietly open, and he caught the device as it dropped. It had kept the door open even though apparently locked.

He walked into the dim foyer and the full range of the Fifth's last movement. Even the house's timbers seemed to vibrate with the German composer's rich, soaring music.

Carter crept from room to room, past the stereo system in the living room, the musty draperies, flocked wallpapers, bookcases, framed oval portraits, antique cut glass and crystal of another time until at last he found what he'd only hoped for.

A door at the end of the foyer hallway, and the small man's voice coming faintly from the other side, drowned by the music.

Carter took out a small cup of specially produced sound-conducting materials created by AXE scientists. He put it against the door and laid his ear on its cool surface.

The man's voice was instantly clear.

"Very good, sixteen," he said in English. "Keep along the same line." There was a pause. "Twelve, your transport is ready in Ankara,'' he went on in French. His voice was assured. His disguise as a distracted scholar hid an efficient, dedicated mind that showed strong in his clipped tones. "Fifteen," he said in German, "the target has changed schedule and will not leave Moscow until the twelfth. Regroup and await further instructions." Another pause. "Success on Damascus road," he continued in English again, "but unit has been rendered inoperative." There's some cause for alarm. We're closely monitoring the situation." Another pause, and this time there was a shuffling of papers. "Zambia success remains quiet," he said in German again. "Don't move. Contact is being arranged."

Carter had heard enough. He pointed Wilhelmina.

He turned the knob, slammed the door open.

The man jerked up his head. He had been sitting hunched over a computerized radio system, sheaves of notes in his hands. His eyes widened in surprise as he stared at Carter and then at the Luger.

"That's the end of today's communications," Carter said in English. "I'll take those."

He picked the notes from the man's hands. The scholarly man's fingers twitched, pulled at the front of his cotton shirt.

"You're back," he said as if informing himself.

"We'll begin at the beginning," Carter said. "What's the name of your organization?"

The man's watery blue eyes narrowed. He started to smile.

Carter grabbed his jaw, pried the teeth apart.

"No you don't! No biting down on poison embedded in your teeth! You'll live longer, and we'll get to the bottom of this!"

The man struggled, swinging a hand awkwardly up toward the AXE agent's face.

Carter shook his head and ducked.

The hand swung by, landed on the man's neck, and scratched vigorously.

"Dammit!" Too late, Carter understood. He clapped the man's hand away.

The man gasped, then went limp in the chair. Blood trickled from the skin on his neck. Before Carter's fast reflexes could catch him, he was dead.

"Hell!"

Carter lowered the small man to the floor just as Beethoven's Fifth crashed to a climactic, ringing end. He heard the great finale without thinking about it, his attention riveted to the dead man, to the lost information. He'd have to do a thorough search of the house.

The pain was sudden. A blow to the back of the head. He was still leaning over when it struck.

It wasn't the first time he'd been hit like that, and in the last fragments of his consciousness, he hoped it wouldn't be the last.

Then the cold blackness engulfed him, threw him into a void of sharp pain. He waded through the delirium of a transitory death.

EIGHT

The room was ice cold. It was night. Carter sensed the darkness. He had no evidence other than the cold, clammy feel of the air and the suggestion within him of empty, lost hours.

As he regained consciousness, he kept his eyes closed and his head dangling low. He was gagged and tied to what felt like a straight-backed chair. The ropes were tight. They cut into his flesh with a professional authority that said he'd never escape. His hands and feet were numb. He was chilled, even though his jump suit was made of special heat-retaining fabric. The rag in his mouth tasted faintly of motor oil. His head pounded dully with the tenacity of a toothache.

The pain was great, but he told himself it was unimportant. What mattered was that he'd failed. The bitter taste of his momentary lack of attention turned to bile. The radio man had killed himself, and then Carter had been knocked out and captured. Neither should have happened.

He must recoup his losses and gain some advantage from the present situation.

He listened to voices that droned in a language he couldn't

recognize, the syllables indistinct, muffled by distance or walls.

He raised his head and opened his eyes.

"He's awake!"

The man called in English toward the only door in the windowless room. His speech had the musical cadence of a Canadian. He sat across from Carter on another straight-backed chair, a Russian AK-47 standing upright and ready between his legs. He'd been reading the Romanian communist party daily *Scinteia*.

He dropped the paper under his chair, reached across, and pulled out Carter's gag. About twenty-five years old, he had a smooth, lineless face and angry eyes.

The door opened. He glanced at it, then gazed at Carter. His eyes flashed.

"Bucharest claims one of their Politburo members was deliberately assassinated a couple of days ago," he told Carter. "You wouldn't happen to have been in Budapest then, Gellért Hill?"

"Andy!"

An older man and a young woman with a stunning, sculptured face entered the small, icy room. They were bundled like Andy in heavy coats, pants, and boots. The man carried an AK-47, and the woman had a Walther.

"Who are you?"

The old man, too, spoke to Carter in English, but his accent was Slavic, perhaps Polish. He was bald with a fringe of gray hair that had been trimmed neatly over his ears. His skin was pink, flushed with the cold, and his eyes burned as if on a quest.

"I assume you heard me swearing," Carter said. "That's why the English."

The older man's eyes blinked slowly in appreciation of Carter's deduction. During stress, ninety-nine times out of a hundred, a person cursed in his native language.

"Very good," the man said. "What's your name?"

"No need to stand on formality," Carter said, smiling. His lips were stiff from the cold. "I don't insist. Go ahead. Introduce yourselves."

The young man lifted his AK-47 to his eye. He aimed it at Carter.

"Andy!"

The older man pushed his jacket sleeve up his arm irritably. His authoritative tones had stopped the young, impetuous man. A glance of frustration escaped Andy's outraged eyes. The older man rubbed his arm, pulled his sleeve down, and frowned.

"Jurgen."

The woman crooked her finger, and the older man leaned toward her. She whispered in his ear. He nodded.

"Of course, Annette." He looked again at Carter. "Why did you kill Heinrich?"

"Heinrich?"

"The man in the radio room."

Carter watched the woman called Annette as she waited for his answer, and suddenly his capture made sense.

"You're not with them," Carter decided.

"Who?"

She had bright, intelligent eyes, but there was an emotionless quality of disinterest or too-early jading.

"He killed himself," Carter told her.

She watched him a moment, then nodded. She wasn't disinterested. She was jaded. Life had taught her lessons she hadn't wanted to learn. But once known, they couldn't be forgotten, and her illusions were forever destroyed. The knowledge made her unhappy but powerful. She was the leader of the trio.

"A capsule on the teeth?" she said, speaking with the clean accent of the American Midwest.

"Something different. Never seen it before."

"The scrape on the neck then," she said. "Must have been embedded next to the jugular. The poison would go directly into the bloodstream."

"Instant death," Carter agreed.

Her cold blue eyes considered him. Her features had once been soft, but life had focused them into a haunting sharpness. She was in her late twenties, a curly-haired blonde, a few tendrils dangling invitingly from beneath a black knit cap.

"You're one of the terrorists," she accused.

"What?"

"A murderer. Why do you kill prominent leaders?"

He laughed.

"So that's what you think."

"Can you prove any different?" she asked scornfully.

"We're on the same trail, hunting the same killers," he said. "At first, I thought you were with them too. My name's Nick Carter, CIA."

He gave her his cover identification and numbers. With a simple telephone call, anyone with connections could substantiate that he was a certified, honorable member of the U.S. international intelligence agency.

Annette pursed her lips, then nodded briskly at Andy and the older man. They left to make the call, and she sat in Andy's chair. She balanced the Walther over her arm, wary and distant.

"Been in the business long?" Carter said conversationally.

She stared coldly, expressionlessly, at him.

"If you're going to do this kind of work," he said, "you

need to maintain a certain sense of humor."

She looked through him as if he didn't exist.

He repressed a smile.

"The other kids won't play with you," he warned. "The teachers will complain."

"Do all CIA men carry so much equipment?" she asked abruptly. "A bomb, knife, and Mercedes?"

Her expression didn't change. If she knew she had a sense of humor, she wasn't admitting it.

"Just what the job calls for," he said. "How about you Israelis?"

Now she stared at him directly, dismayed. He had her attention.

"How did—"

"I know?" he finished. "Not too difficult. You three are different nationalities, and Israel is homeland to the Jews of the world. And then, your older friend has a habit . . . in poker, we'd call it a tell. I had another friend once who did the same thing. He unconsciously rubs the number tatooed on the inside of his arm. The one he got in one of Hitler's death camps. It reminds him of who he is, and that he survived for a reason."

"Very clever, Killmaster."

It was Carter's turn to be surprised, and he allowed himself a rueful smile.

"How long have you known?"

"Long enough. You confirmed it when you gave your name and that phony CIA cover."

"Then how about taking these ropes off?"

"You'll have to tough it out." She offered no apology. "I'll wait until the phony cover—and your actual whereabouts—are confirmed. Wouldn't want to make a mistake at this point."

She almost smiled, pleased, then resumed her cool watch-fulness.

"Have a nice trip from Jerusalem?" he went on. "How are Chaim Herzog, Menachem Begin, Meir Kahane . . . all the boys?"

She didn't move.

"I assume you're on assignment for the Israeli secret service, although with those Russian AK-47s, it does make me suspicious. Do you hunt Nazis, too?"

No response.

"What the hell kind of Jewish name is Annette?"

She bristled.

"I'm French and American, too!"

"Oh," he said and grinned.

The time passed slowly. There was no sound in the small room except for an occasional creak of her chair as she crossed her legs or adjusted her weight. Outside, a mountain wind moaned through the fir trees.

Inside, their breaths made steamy clouds in the air. It was cold enough now that breathing was painful. A cold spring night in the mountains. Carter's head was better, though, and his disposition was improving.

When at last heavy footsteps sounded outside, stamped, a door opened and closed, and when the door to Carter's room opened, he was bored and ready for action.

"Jurgen?" she said, looking at the older man.

"It's as he said," Jurgen replied.

His burning eyes moved from Annette's face to Carter's. There was almost a smile on the somber face, a smile of anticipation. Now they could get to work.

"Very well. Untie him, Andy. We'll go now."

The young man unknotted Carter's ropes.

"Which one of yours did they kill?" Carter asked.

"Daniel Gaban."

"The former prime minister," Carter said thoughtfully. "I read he had a heart attack."

"It was a bomb attack," Jurgen said bitterly. "While he was having breakfast. Gaban was a great patriot."

Carter stood up and rubbed his legs and arms to restore circulation.

"A violent anti-Arab fire-eater," Carter corrected.

"A savior!" Jurgen stepped forward, his hands white on his AK-47, his face flushed. "A leader in the Irgun!"

Annette gripped his arm. His burning eyes glared at her. She shook her head and yanked on the arm. His face softened back to sanity.

"His death started you on the trail?" Carter continued.

"We surrounded the assassin," Annette said, "but before we could close in, he shot himself in the head and died. He'd left a death paper on the gate, similar to a paper left at another death site earlier that week. We never found out who killed the first man, but this time we were able to discover where the assassin lived. He'd been careful to have no identification on him, and he was a foreigner—a Czech—so not known by our usual sources. We circulated his photo, and a teen-ager from one of our youth groups remembered seeing him at a market. He was having trouble figuring out shekels. We traced him back to a rented room. He'd lived Spartanly, but we found the Lübeck address concealed in his papers."

"And then you found me," Carter said. "Is it safe to go back to the house?"

"Jurgen?" Annette said.

"Marsha says no one has arrived."

"Then we go," the Israeli leader said.

The quartet moved through the door and into the rustic living room of a mountain cabin. Andy handed Carter his Luger, stiletto, and gas bomb, and they went out into the cold starry night. They walked single file down a steep trail lit only by moonlight. The cabin quickly disappeared behind them, swallowed by the thick firs. The wind was dying, the trees swaying in a quiet dance. Below and off in the distance, occasional car lights sparkled through the trees.

After about a hundred yards, they came to a clearing. The Mercedes and a Ford Pinto waited. As Carter pulled a heavy coat from the trunk, Annette and Jurgen got into the Mercedes, and Andy into the little Pinto. Warming quickly, the American agent sat in the driver's seat, turned on the heat and motor, and drove out of the clearing. Andy followed in the Pinto.

Annette directed Carter to drive back up the mountain and across a saddle ridge.

"You've been here a while," he observed as the car wound along the road.

"A week," she said. "From the cabin we could watch the house. No one except Heinrich came or went. He puttered in the garden, shopped in Lübeck. We could even see him dusting that awful old furniture through the windows."

"Was the house his?"

"In his name, at least."

"Did you talk to him?"

"Jurgen did."

"He talked about geraniums and Proust," Jurgen offered.

In the rearview mirror, Carter could see the former concentration camp victim shrug.

"I invited him to have a beer with me, and when the check came he wanted to pay it. What kind of murderer is that? I didn't think he had a damned thing to do with assassinating Gaban until he killed himself. And then we saw all that radio equipment."

"He knew a lot," Carter said, and he described the orders he heard Heinrich giving over the radio.

"Merde!" Annette swore softly. "The papers!"

"Marsha took them," Jurgen reassured her. "They've already gone to Haifa."

"Anything on them?" Carter asked, remembering that once he'd held Heinrich's sheaf of notes in his own hands.

"Our code specialists think they were simply personal notes to himself. Agents' numbers and locations. No names. No addresses. No actual events listed. We're testing paper and ink, and our cipher experts are going over them too. It's an intriguing problem."

"But without much hope," Carter said, catching a flash of Jurgen's hot eyes.

"Unfortunately true," the Israeli agent agreed.

At last, Andy trailing in the Pinto, they drove up the steep drive to the Hessian house. A tall regal woman stepped from the shadows, an M-16 over her shoulder, a walkie-talkie in her gloved hand.

"Anything, Marsha?" Jurgen asked.

"Very quiet," the woman said. "Not even the telephone rang."

"Good. Sit in the Mercedes. Get warm."

The four other agents moved into the dark house and, room by room, beginning with the radio room, searched through the bookcases, closets, cupboards, sideboards, tables, desks. They worked for four hours. There was much clutter but little information. It was as if the people who had lived in the house over the years had decided to leave only impersonal litter as their contribution to the house's character. There were no letters or cards, no diaries, no thank-you notes, no lovingly collected names, telephone numbers, or addresses.

But in the radio room there was a metal wastepaper basket whose bottom was covered with an inch of ashes. The scholarly Heinrich must have committed to memory whatever information he had needed, and then burned incriminating messages, addresses, and names. It was a tedious system, but secure. Particularly if you had a poison capsule buried next to your jugular.

"We don't even know their organization's name!" Andy said at last in exasperation.

Annette studied Carter as they stood in the foyer.

"It was a good try," he said, smiling, and extended a hand.

She shook it, her grip strong, and looked directly into his eyes. For a moment he felt the heat of her sexuality. It made him catch his breath.

Quickly she withdrew behind her aloof curtain.

"Where will you go?" she said.

"Don't worry," he said. "I don't know anything more than you do. You can waste one of your personnel if you like. Have me followed."

"Maybe I will," she said and frowned.

He laughed.

"Lady," he said, "I'm glad we're on the same side."

"Are we?" she said.

He laughed again and walked out the door.

"Sorry, Marsha," he said and opened the Mercedes's door. "My turn."

The aristocratic woman bowed her head in acceptance, and slid across the seat and out the door. She disappeared like a willowy wraith into the shadows of the tall pines.

Carter started the big Mercedes, listened to the smooth motor a moment, then drove back down the drive.

This time he had to find a better place to park, a place where no one could see the car.

NINE

Nick Carter piled pine branches thick over the Mercedes to prevent the chrome and glass from reflecting light when caught in the headlights of a car. Above him, the stars twinkled and the cold wind rustled through the mountain's treetops.

Once satisfied the Mercedes was well hidden, he struck off back up the mountain, climbing over the rough terrain with only the moon to guide him. Small invisible rodents scurried through the duff. Far off, an animal snarled and another chattered nervously.

The house was as he'd left it, dark and imposing. He stood quietly under a fir and listened. At last he heard the soft footsteps of the sentry Marsha. She was behind the drive now.

Carter skirted the house and came in silently at the back. He slipped up to the back door, used his set of keys, and entered the black house. He turned on a narrow-beamed flashlight for a fraction of a second. Once he was certain where he was, he turned the beam off and moved through the kitchen, past the counters, appliances, table, and chairs, and to the hall.

He felt the flocked paper with his hand and followed the

hallway, counting doors. The house creaked with the wind. Somewhere a shutter banged.

At last he opened the door to the radio room, closed it, and turned on the light. It was a windowless room, cramped, shiny with computerized equipment.

He walked directly to the radio sender and picked it up. There was nothing on the table below, but taped to the underside of the sender was a photograph.

When Carter had first seen the white edge of the photo earlier during the search with the Israelis, he hadn't known what it bordered. But it was hidden, so he'd known it was important. He'd wanted to see it alone before he decided what to do. Now he looked at the picture with growing excitement.

In the photo were David Sutton, the scholarly man Heinrich, a third man who looked Slavic, possibly Russian, and a fourth man wearing a tuxedo.

The Englishman Sutton had his arm draped over the Slav's shoulder in an act of camaraderie. The four men were sitting at a table in what looked like a sleazy, crowded saloon. The print of the scene was wrinkled, the photographic paper showing white where the photo had been crumpled and then smoothed flat again. It looked about a year old, a treasure that even the dedicated, safety-conscious Heinrich couldn't sacrifice. In the end, it was the emotions that mattered to all humans.

The sound was small, wood scraping against wood.

Carter hit the light switch, stepped behind the door, and slid the photo inside his jacket.

He waited.

The footsteps crept down the hall, stopped as if to think or listen, then disappeared.

He waited longer, sweat beading on his forehead.

At last he opened the door. And smiled.

The footsteps had disappeared because they had gone inside another room and the person had closed the door. A faint line of gray light showed beneath the door, not enough light for it to be a room's light, but instead a small flashlight.

He moved quietly across the room, taking out Wilhelmina. He turned the knob, then slammed open the door.

She whirled around.

It was Annette. A knife glinted in one hand. The flashlight glowed in the other.

"You!" she breathed.

"Delighted to see you again," he said.

She swung the flashlight and closed in with the knife.

He kicked the flashlight from her hand, ducking the knife.

The flashlight skidded across the room and crashed against a table.

"Good commando training," he observed from the dark shadows.

She spun on her heel and slammed the light switch. The room blazed with light. It would glow through the windows and alert the sentry, but the way Annette had been sneaking around, she didn't want anyone to know she was back.

"What about Marsha?"

"Marsha's gone."

She circled him, backing, one step at a time, her cold blue eyes never leaving his.

"You sent her away," he said. "Worried someone in your group is a traitor?"

"You should have left when you had the chance."

"Look, Annette," he said, exasperation starting to grow, "I'm the one with the gun."

"I'm not dead yet."

She lunged, cold eyes alight. The violence—the actual *doing* of something concrete at last—excited her. Passivity was boring, numbing, and she was overdue from her long watch and keeping the others in line.

THE EXECUTION EXCHANGE

She was unstoppable by most standards.

He grinned, and sidestepped. Grabbed the shoulder that was aimed to knock him flat. Caught her thigh with the top of his foot. Spun her.

But she expected it. A damned good commando.

She angled the spin directly into his legs. A mass of whirling energy. Destroyed his balance.

He toppled. But came down on her.

The knife lashed up.

He knocked the knife into a spin across the room.

She glared, angry and frustrated. Sweat moist and shining covered her forehead.

He yanked off the cap. She didn't try to stop him. Blond curls showered to her shoulders.

He looked directly into her deep blue eyes and saw the iciness of distance, the heat of passion.

With the point of her pink tongue, she licked lips suddenly gone dry.

She had a beautiful face, haughty, intelligent. The skin was smooth, rosy with exertion. She smelled of excitement and spice-scented soap.

He wanted her, felt the desire for this arrogant, beautiful woman charge him heavy with need.

He wrapped a hand around the back of her neck, under the curls. He pulled her forward. He wanted her, and he knew she wanted him.

Her lips were inches from his.

Her breath fresh, hot. The lips parted.

Her head arched back below his, the lips open, breathing.

The Israeli woman's eyes flashed with memories. Resisting not him, but herself. Fingernails lashed up to scratch his face.

Quick as a cobra, he caught the hand and pushed her down flat to the carpet.

She moaned. The hand opened as if it had a will of its own.

Moved up his chest, kneading.

"You bastard!" she suddenly cried, her face flushed, violent with acknowledgment of her own need.

She tore at the zipper of his jump suit. He smelled the leather of her boots, and pulled them off.

She watched him with blazing eyes, panting, sweating, now begging with small animal sounds.

Himself naked, he undressed her in a frenzy. She grabbed his hips and pulled him toward her. He shoved into her, and they rocked on the carpet, shouting their explosions, tied together for that moment in eternity.

Afterward, she turned on the room's heater. He put Mahler's Fifth Symphony on the stereo. They pulled cushions from chairs and sofas onto the floor and lay on them without touching one another, still strangers, perhaps even personal enemies, united only by intimacy of the flesh. Gustav Mahler's philosophical, physical music swelled in the air.

The sex was a momentary aberration, her eyes seemed to say to him. Seldom did she decide to indulge, but when she did it was because of fleeting need. He shouldn't take it as anything more than that. Lust.

They smoked, the smoke and steam from their breaths and bodies mingling in the room's warming air. They inhaled and exhaled silently, studying one another with the same suspicions, but now also with the memory of the resentment once between them.

She had a beautiful body, long and lean. He could see part of it still, partially hidden beneath the trousers she'd draped over her.

He flicked up her shirt.

They both gazed at her round breast, the soft pink nipple hardening in the still cold room. She seemed curious, as if the breast weren't her own. He touched the end of the nipple, the tiny hard mass beneath the velvet skin.

He rolled the nipple between his thumb and forefinger. She bit her lower lip, still gazing at the breast, mesmerized. Now there was no doubt the breast and nipple were hers. A flush spread across her cheeks.

"Where is it?" he asked.

"What?"

She gave a little gasp as his fingers gently kneaded the nipple higher, sharper, tenser.

"What you came back for," he said.

"I don't know . . . what you . . ."

"Of course you do."

He watched her pupils dilate into the blue irises. He flicked up the other half of her shirt. The other breast's nipple was already erect. He touched it. It throbbed under his finger. He rolled that nipple, too.

Her lips swelled thick with desire. She lifted languid arms.

He ducked. The arms, suddenly sharp weapons, lashed at him.

"You're a son of a bitch!"

He laughed.

Her eyes were not amused. "You found something!" she accused. "You wouldn't have bothered with me otherwise. You wouldn't have thought that I was after something too!"

"Too simple, my dear," he said.

He wanted her again, the need throbbing between his legs, pounding in his head.

He whipped the trousers from her body, searched the pockets, then threw them across the room. He tipped the tall leather boots over and felt inside. He searched her jacket pockets, then the lining. He stripped off her blouse but found nothing in the light fabric.

Nude, she lay there, watching him. A magnet of flesh and hypnotic desire. And she knew it. Liked it. Wanted the torment and fulfillment.

He tossed the blouse aside.

She reared up, nipped his shoulder, and flowed against his chest, the nipples against his skin, teasing.

He held her chin, their lips close, their breath steaming between them.

"We're on the same side," he said, "unless you've turned. Unless you're a double agent."

"I trust no one."

"You can't win without trusting."

"I'm alive."

"That's not always a measure of success."

"I'll find the terrorists myself."

"Will you?" he said, then he lifted the chin and crushed his mouth down on hers.

Her lips parted. Her tongue darted eagerly between his teeth, exploring. She melted against him, honey and sweat, and he rolled her over. Mounted her, a giant stallion and a wild mare, rocking and bucking until they fought to an explosive victory framed in music and lust.

"Tell me, Ice Princess," Carter said as they once more lay smoking on the living room floor of the Hessian house, closer but still not touching, "where do you live in Israel?"

She inhaled deeply, enjoying the flavor of one of Carter's specially made cigarettes.

"Ice Princess, eh?" she said, a controlled smile on her lips.

With her pale blond beauty and light blue eyes against the deep colors of the richly patterned Oriental carpet, she could be a sculpture in ice. And except for sex, her personality, too, with its distance, aloofness, and suspicion was glacier cold.

"Do you mind?" he said, inhaling, catching with the smoke the vibrant, dark chords of Mahler's symphony.

Her eyes flickered with silent amusement.

"Jerusalem," she said. "Our holiest of cities, center for

three of the world's major religions. While I was growing up in Omaha, my parents told me stories about Jerusalem. How we would go there one day, pray at the Western Wall.''

Carter nodded thoughtfully. "One of the most ancient places in Jerusalem. The remains from the outer wall of the Second Temple that Jesus knew. Built by Herod, burned by the Romans in 70 A.D..''

"The legendary Killmaster memory," she said. "Of course, you're right. The Western Wall. But my parents died in an automobile accident, and I was alone. I . . . I grew up fast. Then I immigrated to Jerusalem by myself.''

"In Hebrew, it's Ir Hakodesh. In Arabic, Al-Quds. And to English Christians, it's Jerusalem. If you stayed, you must have found what you wanted there.''

She nodded, gazing at the wood-beamed ceiling as if it were the Mediterranean and she could easily see across it.

"Even the names for the city are beautiful," she said. "They make me think of the harmony of a dozen languages, the pungent aroma of Turkish coffee, the sight of black-robed Franciscan monks, Russian Orthodox nuns, Armenian priests, and Moslem cadis all walking together in peace.''

"But Jerusalem has a history of war.''

She arched her brows, still not looking at him. Her naked body glowed in the room's bright lamplight.

"All wars—all fighting—must stop," she said quietly. "I've dedicated my life to that. Do you know that when General Allenby went to Jerusalem to accept Turkey's surrender at the end of World War One, he got off his horse at Jaffa Gate and walked into Jerusalem on foot like any other pilgrim? He could have ridden in as a conqueror. You see, that's what Jerusalem could mean to all of us, of any faith. Peaceful coexistence. Respect for different ideas and cultures. Respect for lessons of the past. Jerusalem is so very small, any healthy person can walk around the Old City in an hour. Despite its size, which you'd think would only lead to increased tensions, it's truly an ecumenical city. Meuzzin ring out five times a day to call Moslems to prayer. On Sundays, hundreds of Christian church bells ring, too. We have three sabbaths. Friday for Moslems, Friday nights and Saturdays for us Jews, and Sundays for Christians. Yet we do business with one another, live together, pass each other on the street—different religions, different countries, different beliefs. I think we are quite amazing. Jerusalem.''

"Bombs," Carter said. "Terrorist activities. Kahane's vow to kick every Arab out of Israel. The PLO. How do you explain that?''

"I don't," she said, putting out her cigarette and looking at last across to him. "I try to stop it.''

Her skin was still flushed and rosy from sex, but the face and eyes were once again distant and cold. She held herself back. Any cause carried to extremes could open the door for a person to dive headlong into madness, as sometimes Jurgen helplessly did, and Andy might soon with his angry eyes. People who made commitments to life faced frustrations that those who just walked through, put in their time, didn't bother to think, consider, or care, would never face. Now Carter understood her iciness. It made work and survival possible for her.

He stood, walked to his clothes, and got out the photograph he'd found in the radio room.

"You won't decide for yourself—can't, really," he said, "so I'll decide for you."

He handed her the print. She took it, still gazing questioningly at him.

"We'll work together for the time being," he told her, "until we need to go our own ways, or the job is completed."

She didn't answer. Instead, she agreed by studying the photograph. After a while she got up to walk gracefully to the stereo. Next to an ashtray, slid beneath the heavy turntable, was a matchbook. She brought it to him and put it in his hand.

"I hid it when we were searching," she explained simply.

She sat beside him again, her naked arm against his. He smelled her womanly scent. Mahler's haunting symphony started its fifth and final movement. Together the two agents studied the clues.

The matchbook was from Werner Hall in Prenzlauer Berg, East Berlin. A large hawk with raised wings decorated the cover. Instantly Carter focused on the photo of the four men in the sleazy club. He laughed. She looked more closely, seeing it too. She shook her head.

The table around which the four men were gathered contained three ashtrays, two full of cigarette butts. The third was clean, not yet used. On it was the same hawk as on the matchbook.

Now Carter knew where Sir David Sutton and his three friends—or his three closely watched enemies—had been when the photograph was taken. East Berlin, capital of the German Democratic Republic, behind the Berlin Wall.

TEN

In just twenty-four hours in August 1961, Russian and German communists built a hundred-mile-long wall around the entire city of West Berlin, isolating it a hundred miles from the protection of West Germany, encircling its people with shock and a resignation that even today occasionally burst into homicidal anger among both East and West Berliners.

Nick Carter thought about this as he and the Israeli agent Annette Burden walked down a quiet street in East Berlin's working-class district of Prenzlauer Berg. Called the "antifascist protective barrier" by the East, the prisonlike Berlin Wall's defenses included floodlights, trip alarms, barbed wire, long upturned spikes, electric fences, trained attack dogs, and concrete guard towers manned by *Grenztruppen*—armed border troops—at firing-range intervals.

The "referendum of the feet" that frightened the communists into building the deadly wall—three million people had fled the East, about half of them through West Berlin—had now decreased. Now only twelve a month tried to escape. Some still succeeded. A new generation had grown to adulthood with the familiar gray wall in their backyard. And as life in East Germany improved, those living under the yoke of communism found the shackles less burdensome, the benefits increasing, and a dangerous, uncertain escape far too great to risk.

Carter and Annette walked side by side, hands in pockets in the chilly spring evening. The air was acrid with the smoke of brown coal. At the corner ahead, a policeman standing duty in a yellow pool of lamplight shifted his weight. His jackboot scraped the grit-covered sidewalk. Pedestrians strolled by him, their clothes drab, out-of-date, but neatly pressed. They nodded politely. Children walked with them, respectful, well mannered, in a divided city proudly twenty-five years behind its flashy, gaudy, uppity, sister city West Berlin.

"Another block," Annette observed quietly, her long, lanky stride certain beside Carter's.

Carter nodded down the street.

"You can see the sign now," he said. "Under the street light. Werner Hall."

Their passage into the city had been uneventful, the Quadripartite Agreement of 1971, excellent passports supplied by AXE, and their remarkable acting skills smoothing the few suspicions of the armed border guards who had been instructed to welcome visitors who came to spend money in a communist nation poor by Western standards.

Nick Carter considered the city—and the nation—he had entered. It was all part of the careful preparatory work that kept him alive and brought him his legendary high success rate.

There were few signs, in this old-fashioned, mixed commercial and residential area that they were walking through, of East Berlin's reputation as the most prosperous city in Eastern Europe. The city had grown and rebuilt itself from a 1945 low point when more than half of all its apartments were destroyed and a billion cubic feet of rubble clogged its streets. Now shiny highrises, chrome-and-glass apartments, and the spacious Alexanderplatz plaza for trade and tourism highlighted what the city's communist neighbors regarded as the Paris of the East.

The working-class street that Carter and Annette strolled through displayed little evidence of this progress. A relic largely unchanged since World War II, the old, shabby neighborhood of tall brick apartment houses and age-thickened, gnarled trees was still scarred by the wounds of the war's bombing.

Trash lay in a heap behind a parked car. Above, a woman stood at a lighted window, a Strauss waltz playing the cornices and concrete ledge around her blasted away forty years ago in an Allied bombing raid. The government was struggling with housing, the worst being taken care of first, as it focused on a 1990 goal of three hundred thousand new and renovated apartments. As always, hope was the carrot dangled in front of the slow-moving donkey.

Carter and Annette walked on down the sidewalk, paused at the corner, and smiled at the young police officer who looked right through them, well aware of the importance of a police state. They moved on, two hard-working East Berliners out for an innocent night's entertainment at Werner Hall.

They followed the sign's painted arrow that pointed down a steep sidewalk staircase that smelled pungently of mold and ale. The bright, cheerful sounds of laughter, talk, and expertly played polka music resounded in the narrow passageway.

"Of course it's better for me than it is for the Bulgarians," the man inside the door was saying as Carter and Annette entered. The polka music and laughter were instantly louder. "I'm a German," he went on. "We East Germans, we have it good."

"Two," Carter told him.

The man looked briefly at him but studied Annette. He was a big man with broad, heavy shoulders. He opened and closed his hands absentmindedly, the meaty muscles on his arms bulging beneath a light cotton shirt. He was the bouncer, and he liked the work.

He raised one of the hands and snapped the fingers, his eyes never leaving Annette. Carter felt her move restlessly beside him. He put an arm over her shoulder and pulled her roughly to him. The bouncer blinked. He might be slow, but even he could figure that out.

"Stupid Poles," he continued to his friend over the lively music. The friend wore a soft brown felt hat perched on the back of his head. "Why do they want to strike? When you're a worker, you've got to work."

A sweating, buxom waitress came toward them carrying a fistful of beers in one hand and an order pad in the other.

"Two?" she said and walked off without waiting for an answer.

As the agents followed the heavyset waitress, Carter heard the reply from the man wearing the soft felt hat.

"Their standard of living is going backward in Poland," he said thoughtfully, explaining it both to the bouncer and to himself. "Nothing like the progress here." ·

"Ignorance," Annette fumed in a low voice next to Carter's ear as they sat at a round wooden table next to a pillar.

The waitress plopped the four beers on a nearby table, the foam sloshing up the sides of the big mugs then settling down into tall heads without spilling a drop.

Carter put a cautionary hand on Annette's arm, looked up at the waitress, and ordered two beers.

"Ignorance," Annette went on, glaring at the overworked waitress's back as she bustled away. "It's the best defense any government has. Fool the people, and you've got carte blanche to do whatever you like!"

"Your anger is showing," Carter said, smiling into her indignant beauty. "Careful. You'll be mistaken for human."

"Ha!" she said, compressing her lips. "We've work to do."

"Glad you reminded me. Might have forgotten."

"Don't humor me, Carter. It's a waste of effort."

He grinned and shook his head. She was alternately desirable and hopelessly irritating, and even when she was irritating, she was desirable. When she unveiled her cold eyes long enough for him to see, he knew she was as attracted to him as he was to her. And perhaps even more puzzled by him.

Carter and Annette went back to work.

They gazed nonchalantly around the room, the two remaining unidentified men in Heinrich's photograph burned in their memories: the Slavic-looking one with David Sutton's arm thrown casually over his shoulder, and the man in the tuxedo.

The warehouse-size room was a single, large hall with the center filled with long tables seating up to sixteen each, and small round and square ones along the perimeter of the room. The decorations were old. Pre-World War II paintings of the Bavarian countryside, crossed Prussian swords with dangling faded red tassels, stuffed deer and wild boar heads with the glazed eyes of death's defeat, and ornate gold filigreed mirrors that reflected across the half-full room. A film of dust and grease seemed to cover everything. The decorations gave the hall a sense of musty oldness, as if the past were a walking corpse.

To their right was a raised stage on which the polka band in short pants and embroidered shirts played their lively tunes. Below them, another band stood on break, drinking beer from steins and talking in each other's ears. Couples, families, and friends sat in clumps at tables throughout the warm hall, laughing, drinking toasts, tapping their feet.

"I don't see either of them," she said at last.

"Not yet."

He picked up the ashtray, noting the raised wings of the hawk. She nodded. They were in the right place. They lit cigarettes, smoked, talked infrequently, bored as if they had been together so long that animated conversation between them had died a natural death.

The polka band ended its set and people looked up expectantly for the next entertainment. A knife thrower bounded out onto the stage, brandishing long knives that caught the overhead lights and glinted menacingly. The audience loved him, clapping enthusiastically, and he threw each knife with solemnity at a half-naked girl, flourishing the weapons so that the pleased audience would be certain that only his superb skill kept the trembling girl from instant death. He ended his show to thunderous applause, and the emcee beamed and clapped too.

In between musical breaks by the combo on the floor, the announcer brought on a memory expert in all the great Germanic wars, then a group of four young girls in frilly white aprons who yodeled, and last a man who played the xylophone with his hands while one foot beat a floor drum.

The audience booed the xylophone player. One red-faced man yelled that the music sounded as if it were made by a broken washing machine. Immediately the emcee's hook shot out from the side of the stage and dragged the embarrassed amateur off. The audience loved that, and clapped and stamped its feet. Being judge and jury pleased them, especially if their decision was instantly and painlessly carried out. People liked to keep their own hands clean.

"Three hours," Annette observed impatiently. "Not a sign of either of them."

Across the room, the bouncer still occasionally studied Annette, and she would glare back at him. Being on watch was boring, but at least they were inside, warm, where there was beer and something to do besides count the seconds in a minute.

People came and went. Sweating waitresses balanced full mugs of beer to the tables and carried off empty ones by the trayful. The musicians played. The entertainers did their acts with varying degrees of success. Men flirted with women. Women hid their interest behind fluttering, work-worn hands and shy glances.

And Carter and Annette watched.

Another hour passed, then two.

Near midnight, a new act ran out onto the stage. It was a magician, carrying a black-draped table, wearing a tuxedo shiny with age.

Carter and Annette continued to smoke quietly. Nothing about them gave away their excitement.

The magician was the man in the tuxedo in Heinrich's photograph.

But now, besides the tuxedo, he wore a large red spot painted festively on each cheek as if he were a cabaret entertainer from long ago. He had a long, boneless face, and was tall and rangy. And now that Carter saw him in person, saw the way he moved, heard the timber of his voice, he realized he'd met the man before.

In Budapest, the man dressed in an expensive business suit had tried to hire Carter's taxi to take him to a fashionable address—14 Józsefhegyi Street on Rose Hill—while Carter was in disguise tailing the double agent József Pau. The man had spoken Hungarian like a native. Now he spoke working-class German as if he were to the factory born.

Carter edged behind Annette. If he recognized the magician, the magician might recognize him.

"What's wrong?" she whispered, glancing at Carter, then she followed his gaze back to the stage where the magician busily waved a wand over his upturned top hat.

Carter explained quickly, and a triumphant smile of confirmation spread across her beautiful, cold face.

"You stay here," he told her before she could object.

He stood, turned, and walked around the perimeter of the room, his head ducked in defeat, his hands dug deep into his pockets, his feet shuffling as if life were drudgery, and work a punishment for living. People, made uncomfortable by the emotions his presence raised, averted their eyes when he passed. It was a good disguise. No one wanted him near, and they'd forget him as soon as possible.

He walked to a door marked rest rooms, glancing over his shoulder once to see Annette alone at their table, smoking furiously.

The door opened into a corridor, just as he'd suspected. Two of the doors along the hall were marked for rest rooms, another was labeled Office, a third that swung busily back and forth was obviously a kitchen. Costumed singers, comedians, and musicians prowled the corridor, smoking, drinking, chattering to keep away their stage nerves.

Carter paced the length of the hall, his hands behind his back. He found the men's dressing room at the end of the corridor, down another flight of stairs. It would be a dank hole down there.

Carter paused at the top of the stairs, lit a cigarette, and listened to the shouts of laughter and applause that accompanied another of the magician's tricks.

Across from the stairs was a small square of royal purple curtain. He drew back the musty velvet cloth. Through a darkened pane of glass he saw the stage and audience. From here, the next act could gauge the reception awaiting them.

The magician was finishing his act, bowing to endless applause, while across the crowded room Annette's eyebrows were raised in scorching dismissal of the persistent bouncer who hovered over her like a dog salivating over a bone. Carter allowed himself a brief smile. The bouncer was in over his musclebound head.

Next to the window was the stage door through which the magician would exit. Carter backed off, now certain that there were only three exits. The first exit was the front door where Carter and Annette had entered the bar. The second was the side door that backed next to the top of the stairs down to the men's dressing room; it would be the stage door. And the third would be through the back of the kitchen.

It was simple to deduce that the magician would probably go out the stage door, but as a second choice he might exit through the kitchen where he could avoid the clamoring throng from the hall.

Carter ground out his cigarette on the wood floor already scarred by thousands of other cigarette burns made by waiting performers, and assumed his hunched walk to return to the table.

The audience was already back to their beers, eager for the next act. Ahead, Annette was staring coldly into empty space, a hand crushing a pack of cigarettes.

The bouncer passed Carter on his way back to the front door. Startled, he recognized Carter, gave him a guilty look of pity, and hurried to the safety of guarding the front door. There a man knew his friends, and the women, although not stunning, at least were grateful for a real man's attention.

"You've charmed another admirer," Carter said, smiling as he sat next to her. She was remarkable, admirable, and a constant challenge.

"Moronic ox," she muttered grumpily and drank her beer. "Are we set?"

He told her the location of the doors. They stood, leaving money on the table. She rested her head on his shoulder, a little drunk, and he supported her to the front door. The bouncer turned his back, disgusted, but at least now he had an explanation for her rejection. His pride was saved, and he leaned over earnestly in conversation with the man who wore the soft felt hat.

Outside, the street was almost deserted. A new policeman was on duty in the lamplight a block away. The air was sharp with the fresh bite of spring. The stars twinkled overhead as if preserved forever under clear glass.

Standing on the sidewalk just above the Werner Hall's front entrance, Carter and Annette took in their surroundings, noting the paths of the few pedestrians and the slow-moving cars, then split up.

He watched her for a moment, seeing her walk confidently down an alley on one side of the building. She had a hand in her coat pocket, and in the pocket was her Walther.

Satisfied, he strode off in the opposite direction, around the tall brick building. The floors above held apartments, often a family of four to a room, one bathroom to a floor, and a coal-burning stove to cook on. Despite guaranteed-for-life jobs and the government's statistical evidence of improving conditions, East Berliners still found the symbolism of the Berlin Wall embarrassing. It was an admission that despite the state's assurances, something was basically wrong with the society. Parents had difficulty explaining the discrepancies—particularly the Berlin Wall—to the new generations. For those born to any preordained order, free will was still a characteristic that had to be trained out of people.

The scream was short, hollow. Almost as if it hadn't existed at all.

Carter raced down the alley, his Luger tight in his hand, and rounded the corner.

Annette slammed an elbow deep into the belly of one of her two attackers. He collapsed to his knees, his face blue.

The second man threw a rope around Annette, then yanked her tight into its loop.

She kicked high, her boot reflecting light from the single bulb that glowed above the kitchen entrance she had been watching.

The man with the rope dodged, laughing.

"A tigress! What a waste!"

The other man staggered to his feet.

"Get her money, idiot! Someone will hear!"

"Good thinking," Carter said. "But too late."

He pointed Wilhelmina at the East Berliner holding the rope. Both robbers glared terrified at Carter, ignoring for the moment their prey. Annette was just better dressed enough than most East Berliners to give a man with a state-mandated job of no pay increases the hope of a little extra money. The poor in all nations had dreams. In East Germany, a two-cylinder Trabant car was priced astronomically at $15,000 in American money, and a color television cost between $1,000 and $2,000.

"*Polizei!*" one said hoarsely.

"Not yet," Annette said. "But I'll scream and the one on the corner will be here in ten seconds."

"What . . . what do you want?" the man with the rope said, dropping the rope's end as if it were scorching his hands.

"Well, better ethics would be too much to ask," Carter said. "So I suggest you just leave. Give it up for the night."

"You'll . . . you'll let us go?" said the robber Annette had kicked.

"If you leave now," Annette said, stepping out of the rope. "Immediately."

The two robbers looked at one another, then at Carter and Annette.

"No tricks?" the one with the rope said. "I have a wife, a boy . . ."

"No tricks," Carter said as he began to coil the rope. "Get out of here before I finish with this."

The men exchanged a look of awe at their good fortune. Amateurs, they had not yet developed the professional's thrill of the job itself. They wanted the money and felt only its loss, not the loss of the challenge.

They raced down the alley, their cheap, dark clothes disappearing into the night.

"Thieves," Annette said, disgusted. "Of all the bad luck."

Carter nodded curtly, tossed the rope into a trash container, and slid his Luger back into his pocket.

"Better get back," he said, already retracing his steps to his post.

Annette nodded, then blended deep into the shadows made by stacks of empty wooden crates waiting outside the kitchen.

"I'll be here," she said softly. "Waiting."

He didn't bother to nod, too intent on the door that had gone unwatched for perhaps ten minutes. Long enough for the magician to hurry out of costume, clean his face, dress again, and be long gone from Werner Hall.

Carter's only hope was that the magician had no reason to be in a hurry.

He rounded the corner.

They were waiting for him.

In midstep, the six men pushed him up against the wall.

He grabbed for his Luger.

Two iron hands crushed his arms, lifted him. His feet dangled helplessly a foot above the ground.

"Nice work, Killmaster," said the Werner Hall magician who was also the tall, rangy man with the long, boneless face from Budapest. He'd cleaned off the theatrical paint.

There were five others. One of them was the bouncer. He leered in Carter's face as he held Carter's arms immobile against the brick wall. He had the strength of a bull elephant.

"Perhaps we should hire you to clean up our streets," the

magician went on. "You could reform the criminals at the same time." He took a small object from his sleeve and held it high under the alley's light. It was a syringe.

"Delighted," Carter said. "A wonderful opportunity. We could team up. But you'd have to improve the level of your friends. Muscles on the arms are useful, but between the ears they're subnormal."

The bouncer growled deep in his throat. His broad, flat face turned deep red.

"There's room for all," the magician said soothingly. He pressed the plunger, popping out air bubbles.

"Not for me," Carter said and twisted, kicking against the hands that held him like steel bands. It was an impossible position to kick from.

The magician chuckled.

"Deiter, if you please."

The bouncer gave a cruel smile and released one of Carter's arms to the two hands of one of his comrades. With his free hand, the bouncer grabbed Carter's leg, twisting the thigh.

"Annette!" Carter shouted. "Run!"

"Too late." The magician smiled again. He injected the drug into Carter's leg. "We have her."

He watched Carter's face. A wave of nausea swept over the AXE agent. The magician's face blurred. Carter felt himself falling, falling, although he knew he couldn't be. He tried to swim back up to consciousness. The magician spoke again, this time as if from a distance too great to contemplate.

"And now we have *you*," the magician said. "It's too late, Killmaster. Very much too late."

ELEVEN

The room stank of mold and mildew. Somewhere far off, water dripped slowly. The room itself had the impenetrable silence that came from thick stone, and a deserted feeling that sent chills up Nick Carter's spine.

He didn't know where this place was. All his weapons were gone. He was weak from the drug the magician had injected. His head throbbed painfully. And he didn't like the looks of this stone cell.

It made him think of the fabled, persistent Count of Monte Cristo, this dungeon hole. But even the Count of Monte Cristo would be discouraged by the solid stone coffin Carter and the Israeli agent Annette Burden had been thrown in. Could they escape? Or would they simply be hauled out and killed?

Carter lay on a pile of straw on the floor, holding Annette. She was still unconscious, a curly-haired blonde with a beautiful face, a long, femininely rounded body, and a first-rate mind. Asleep, she was a rosy-cheeked angel. But when she awakened . . . he allowed himself a smile as he contemplated her disposition then.

He lifted her shoulder, lay her arm across her chest, and slid away. She moaned and shook her head. Her lashes made long shadows on her cheeks from the light of the kerosene lantern sitting on the tall wooden boxes behind them.

He checked his twenty-four-hour watch. It was noon. They had been unconscious twelve hours. In the underground, windowless cell, it was impossible to tell the hour without a watch.

He moved around the room, feeling the solid limestone walls. The cell was about ten feet by ten feet. A few prisoners had left thick marks on the walls. Without knives, they'd had to improvise with other instruments, perhaps spoons. The marks showed attempts at initials, hearts, other drawings, even a skull and crossbones. None had had the stamina—or the time—to leave a message.

Just as he'd judged from his bed on the straw, the walls were dishearteningly solid. And the heavy, double-thick, barless, windowless door was built of iron. Encrusted with rust, the door had been there a long time, and from the look of it had never been broken through.

He stopped, resting his forehead against the wall where he'd begun. He felt dizzy and weak. His head throbbed as if he'd been on a two-week drunk. The cold limestone refreshed his painful flesh. He waited until the throbbing lessened, then he started on the ceiling.

It was too high to reach, but he walked along the floor, his head angled back, searching for a crack, a fissure, a darkened line on the limestone to indicate someone long ago had found a way to escape. Again, the ceiling appeared solid. What he was hoping for wasn't likely, but it was possible.

He squatted on the floor and dropped his head down between his knees. His ears rang, and a sharp pain pulsated behind his eyes. He forced himself to breathe slowly and deeply until at last the pain from the drug again lessened.

Now he checked the floor. He crawled on his hands and knees, feeling every grimy inch. Slime grew on some of the stones, probably from an underground spring, maybe related to the distant dripping water whose irritating regularity he refused to be annoyed by.

Again he found nothing. He'd known he wouldn't, but still he'd had to try. A Killmaster didn't give up. Ever.

He sat on his haunches, breathing slowly and evenly, waiting for his head to calm.

At last he stood again and walked to the tall wooden boxes from which the kerosene lantern cast a yellow glow in the dark room. He smiled. Of course. These were two of the crates that had been piled outside the kitchen of the Werner Hall where the two thieves had tried to rob Annette.

And the magician and his friends must have used the boxes to crate Carter and Annette for transportation to his dungeon hole, wherever that was.

"Nick?" Annette's voice was raspy, as if it hadn't been used in a long time.

"Don't sit up," he cautioned, returning to the straw.

"Where the hell . . ."

She gasped and fell back, her hands gripping her head.

"In hell, yes, for all I can tell," he said mildly, then sat beside her on the straw.

"Does it go away?"

"The cell, no. Eventually the headache gets better."

"You're not funny."

"Good. It's not a joke."

Flat on her back, still holding her head, she looked at him. Her blue eyes were bloodshot. Her blond curls were wild with tousling. Sticks of straw stuck out from the tangle of hair. She looked like a sixteen-year-old who had had second thoughts about sacrificing her virginity in the hayloft.

"The least you could've done was not get caught," she griped. "Some Killmaster."

"It's all part of the plan."

She struggled to a sitting position again, squinting her eyes with the pain.

"What plan?" she asked suspiciously.

"A Killmaster *always* has a plan." He smiled as he picked straw from her spun-gold hair. "Didn't you know that?"

"I don't believe you," she decided.

He chuckled, stood up slowly, and walked back to the crates.

"I feel much better already," he told her. "You will soon, too."

He moved his hands over one crate.

"You've checked the cell?" She was making conversation, hiding her fears behind talk. Activity decreased anxiety.

"Everything. Solid as a rock. But then, it *is* a rock. Or carved out of one, at any rate."

She watched him, her arms crossed over her knees.

"We'll jump them when they come back," she told him.

"How do you know they're coming back?" he said, finding a loose board at last. He ripped it off, nails squealing.

"They didn't keep us alive for nothing," she reasoned.

"We don't have any weapons," he said. "Makes it a bit one-sided, doesn't it?" He tore off another piece of the crate.

"What about those boards?" she said, pointing to the two he had pulled off and leaned against the wall. "They're sturdy. We can distract whoever comes, then knock them out."

"Why didn't I think of that?"

He stood back and grinned at her.

"Monster! Bastard! SOB! That's why you pulled them off!"

"You're charming when you're angry."

Enraged, she leaped to her feet. Screamed. Clutched her head. Sank against the limestone wall.

Carter grabbed her by the shoulders and picked her up.

"I told you," he said softly. "Wait. Your head will clear. If you move too rapidly, you'll black out."

"But . . ."

"Hush."

He pressed her to him. She was shivering. A cold sweat glistened on her waxy face.

He lay her on the straw and took off his jacket.

"No," she said.

"Shut up."

He covered her.

But his fingers lingered on the hem of his heavy sheepskin jacket. The fingers remembered what the drugged mind had forgotten.

He found the loop of thread and pulled it carefully.

"What are you doing?"

She was breathing heavily, but her eyes were open. She was unstoppable.

"How do you feel?" he said as a long, paper-thin packet fell into his hand.

"Lousy. What else?"

"An honest woman." He smiled into her blue, bloodshot eyes. "Honest women have always been my downfall."

She sighed, and years of toughened protection sloughed away. Suddenly she was young and vulnerable. A child who'd grown up so fast that the childhood had had to be abandoned unfinished.

She touched his cheek.

"Thank you."

"Stay covered," he said. He kissed the hand and slid it back beneath his jacket.

She smiled wanly and closed her eyes. She would sleep. The best medicine. The magician must have given her a dose as large as Carter's. With her lower body weight, she was having an understandably bad reaction.

He returned to the iron door and opened the packet. Inside were a small lockpick, a file, various medicinal pills in a flat container, compressed pellets that were like miniature hand grenades, and four sheets of paper-backed tape strips.

He peeled off one strip of the tape. Since there was no lock on this side of the door, there was no way to pick it. But the tape would help.

He pressed four strips of the tape in the shape of a rectangle on the door where he estimated a lock should be. He made the rectangle small to conserve on tape. He scratched his thumbnail over the tape, then turned his head.

Instantly he felt the heat and smelled the ozone.

When he looked back, the tape had scorched off and a trench had burned into the thick iron.

He did this five times.

At last the tape ate through, and the piece of iron rectangle fell inside the door that was hollow after all.

But there was no lock. He reached inside the door and felt around. At last he found it, but it was low, out of reach, very close to the ground.

The discovery discouraged him, but it also helped to confirm his suspicions. They were in a structure probably built in the Middle Ages when people were much shorter and locks were not only primitive, but considerably lower. And from the look and smell of this dungeon and the placement of the lock, their prison was probably beneath a castle.

He sat back on his haunches and considered the door. He didn't have enough tape to go through the procedure again to burn out a piece of the iron where the lock was. He didn't want to wait until someone came to get them. Boards didn't appeal to him as the best of weapons.

Weapons. That was it.

He smiled and took out two of the compressed pellets from

the packet. They were miniature hand grenades—not as much punch as the full-size ones, but certainly enough for the job at hand.

He returned to Annette. She'd slept another half hour. He hoped that it was enough.

"Annette."

Color had returned to her face, and she'd moved in her sleep, her face now against the wall, the lamplight making her hair glow like beaten gold.

"How do you feel?"

She opened her eyes and turned to look at him.

"I don't know," she said.

"We're ready to break out, but I don't want to do it until you can at least walk."

"Of course."

She'd learned her lesson. She sat up slowly, breathing deeply. He supported her shoulders.

"I hate being an invalid."

"The weakness will pass."

She nodded and stood. Her legs were wobbly, but she refused to give in to their uncertainty.

"I'm ready," she announced.

"We'll wait until *I* think you're ready."

She glared at him, too drained for the emotion necessary to object.

"How old were you when you emigrated?" he said, wishing he had a cigarette to offer her.

"Sixteen. I went directly to a kibbutz in the Sinai."

"And how old were you when your parents died?"

"Ten. Then I lived with foster families. Some were kind. Some weren't."

He watched her heavy breathing, knowing the effort to talk was exhausting. But it would help clear her head.

"How many foster families?"

"Fourteen." She smiled crookedly. "I wasn't easy. They passed me around."

"You were angry. Angry your parents had died and deserted you to such an insecure, unfriendly future."

She shrugged, a sign she was feeling better. She hadn't noticed the improvement yet.

"I didn't analyze it. When friends of my parents invited me to the Sinai, the agency let me go. They were relieved to be rid of me, I expect."

Her skin color was healthier. Her eyes clearer. Her voice stronger.

"Can you stand away from the wall now?" he asked.

She moved so that her weight was completely on her feet. She blinked her eyes slowly and realized she felt better. She reached up to her hair, touching the stiff straw. She pulled out pieces.

"I must be a mess," she muttered. Then she looked at him. "You're right. I am better. Let's get on with it. What do you have in mind?"

He told her. She nodded crisply, then handed him his jacket.

She returned to the straw and lay flat, face down, arms over her head.

He pulled the tabs on the hand grenade pellets and tossed the little bombs down the door's hole. Then he raced across the room to fall next to her, arms over his head, too.

The impact of the explosion shuddered over them.

Smoke and dust clotted the air. Carter and Annette coughed and looked up.

The way was clear to escape. The thick iron door hung partially open, attached only from the top hinge. The bottom of the door angled sharply up, a hole blasted near the floor. The blast had been large enough to free them, and with the thickness of the castle walls, perhaps small enough that no one else had heard.

Carter and Annette jumped up. He looked once at her and saw that she was well enough now to make herself move fast.

They ran through the churning cloud of dirt particles and out down a long corridor.

"Where to?" she gasped.

"I've been promoted," he said, grinning. "She's actually asking, not telling."

"If you don't have any ideas," she said, ignoring him, "I have a suggestion."

"What?"

"I know this castle. There was part of a drawing on the wall. I saw it when we were talking. I can get us out of here."

Carter nodded.

"Lead on," he said.

They ran on down the moldy corridor, past the trickle that dripped with irritating regularity between limestone blocks, to the corner where the corridor ended in a T.

They slid flat against the wall. No voices. Carter peered around the edge. No one. Their captors trusted the old dungeon to keep the two agents imprisoned.

With Annette in front, they ran on along another corridor, this one with open rooms that had once stored grains, vegetables, cured meats, and coal. At last they came to steps wide enough that six people abreast could comfortably climb them.

Annette pressed a forefinger to her lips and, stealthy as a cat, climbed the stone stairs. Above them, an old embroidered tapestry hung from a wrought-iron staff. They were entering territory where there was a greater chance of discovery.

They moved like shadows along the wall, ducking into a

room behind a closed door as a butler, proper in black tails and starched white shirt, carried a silver tray with a single bottle of Three Turkeys rye like a flagpole in the center.

"Wait," Annette cautioned Carter as he started to move out from the room. "He'll be back."

The room was decorated in watery pastels, the wainscoting pale pink, the walls a washed-out blue. The furniture was light and ornate with spindly legs and graceful curves. A large embroidery hoop was mounted next to a rocking chair. A half-finished forest drawing stood on an easel next to a petit-point chair. There was a harpsichord, a flute, and a rolltop desk displaying a time-faded account book open next to an inkwell. It was the drawing room where long ago the castle's noblewomen had gathered to occupy themselves, manage the estate, and teach the family's young girls the skills necessary to be ladies.

"It's the Van Hornbostel castle," Annette whispered. "A West German historical monument. Owned by a private investment group now but open to tourists every day. Makes money and is a tax write-off."

The implication in her tone was that if the government owned the castle, the money would be going to feed and clothe the poor and not lining the unpatched pockets of the already wealthy.

"You've been here before?" he said.

"I was an art history major. I studied the castle for two weeks. The university in Jerusalem sent me." She watched out the crack of the door. "There goes old Joachim. The butler. It's safe now."

They again ran down the corridor, but this time only to the next door. She paused at the door, and the two pressed their ears to it. There were voices inside, talking in a babble of languages.

She glanced at him, telling him with her eyes to follow

again. They ran lightly twenty paces and turned right beneath an ornate crystal chandelier, down another corridor. This one was short, but it was lined like the others with family portraits, tapestries, and occasional suits of gleaming armor.

"The library," she whispered. "An enormous room. We have less chance of being noticed in this hall. Out of the traffic flow."

Again they pressed ears to the door. The babble of languages was quieting. One voice dominated. A man's. It had an English accent, high-class Oxbridge. A voice Carter recognized. He looked down at the old doorknob and squatted. Yes, the keyhole was large. He peered through and into a room lined with leather-bound books rising from the hand-knotted antique carpet to the arched plaster ceiling. And at the end of a long library table, around which eleven people sat, stood Mr. Justice Paul Stone, the same judge who had been a member of the exclusive luncheon club at Andrea Sutton's Greek restaurant in Soho.

"It is a pity," Stone was saying in his clipped speech, "but we must rid ourselves of the risk if our work is to go on. Andrea has been told. The executioners are on their way."

The men at the table nodded solemnly. They looked like a board of directors accepting the face-saving resignation of someone they'd already fired. The magician, now wearing a natty tweed jacket, was one of them, sitting next to a man in a plain black suit. He was the Slav from Heinrich's photograph. Across from them, sitting with his chair at an angle, was the member of Parliament, William Reid, also from the Soho gathering. He wore a pin-striped suit and rep tie, and blew perfect smoke rings into the air above the table. His aristocratic face was set immobile. He didn't like the decision but accepted the necessity. It was part of taking responsibility for one's beliefs.

"It's all quite legal," Mr. Justice Stone went on. A tall,

thin man with craggy features, he had a face that had seldom had to accept defeat. Life's struggles had been lessons for him in certainty. Philosophy was a game for amateurs, and a real leader knew what was wrong and did something about it. Anyone wanting solutions would be attracted to him, and he would accept their allegiance as his logical reward.

"You were able to draw justice papers on them?" William Reid asked. For a mind that lived by preordained opinions, form was as important as substance.

"Naturally," the justice assured him. "I refer to the law on traitors. If the American and Israeli were merely busybodies, we would be able to distract and diffuse them. If they were foreign spies for a power that had declared war on us, we would have to hold them prisoner until the end of the war. But they supposedly work with and for us. Their aims are the same as ours—peace and justice for all. Nevertheless, they are trying to stop us. They are traitors to our cause. The justice papers have been legally drawn. Death warrants, of course. The two will be executed at twilight. Any questions?"

Carter looked up at Annette.

"You heard?" he asked.

She nodded, her face flushed with anger.

Running feet thundered down the long corridor outside the library's front entrance.

"Our weapons are on the table," he told her. "Can you distract them, get them out of the room? I'll grab our—"

The library door banged open.

"They've escaped!" the voice boomed in German.

Quickly Carter dropped to the keyhole. A second later the dozen men were on their feet, moving toward the door, their faces stretched in alarm.

"Both?" the judge asked the guard who had brought the news.

It was the bouncer from Werner Hall in East Berlin, and with him was another of the men who had captured Carter there.

"They bombed the door!" the bouncer said, his head wagging back and forth as he watched the expensively dressed board of directors flood out the door. "We didn't hear a thing. We'd have heard that, don't you think? A bomb!"

In a natural reaction to any escape, the captors were on their way to the empty cell. It was a fruitless gesture. They should have been formulating a plan to look for the prisoners, but surprise often shocked the sense out of people.

"Gross negligence!" the judge accused the bouncer as he strode last through the door. "You relied on the security of the cell instead of posting a guard!"

The German's head drooped. Guilt spread across his face. Then determination to do better. He followed his employers out and tidily shut the door.

"Wait here," Carter told Annette.

He opened the door, dashed inside, scooped up the Luger, Walther, two knives, his gas bomb, and his gold cigarette case, and ran back to Annette in the side corridor. He shut the door and handed the Walther to the Israeli agent.

She held the gun a moment, her gaze on it as if it were a long-lost lover. Then she checked the chambers, hefted it, and watched Carter do the same with his Luger. They smiled at one another, sharing a conspiracy of relief, then slipped their knives into the secret cases on their arms, and Carter secured his gas bomb on his inner thigh.

"London next," Carter told her as they slipped down the hall. "There's a woman in Soho. Now that I know she has the key, I'll be able to get the information."

"You're sure?" she asked, her eyes narrowed in suspicion.

"Positive."

The two agents stopped at the intersection with the main corridor.

Carter peered around the corner and looked directly into the eyes of the beefy bouncer.

It was an act of chance. At any other time, the East German's gaze would likely have been elsewhere, scanning the corridor, doing his job of guarding now that he had no one to guard but doing it well because Mr. Justice Stone had shamed him.

The bouncer instantly recognized his missing captive. With reflexes trained to act without thinking, he aimed his M-16.

Carter ducked.

The bullet tore out a hole in the wall's edge. Splinters shot like needles through the air. The noise reverberated. Shouts erupted from both ends of the central corridor.

"Damn!" Carter swore.

TWELVE

There was a sudden silence as if the old castle were holding its breath. Then heavily booted feet pounded toward them. The old castle echoed. But the thick floors and walls seemed quietly unmoved, unaffected by the impact of the M-16 blast, the thundering feet, the sense of impending death. History took little notice of the tantrums of the present, mindlessly swallowing the spilled blood of the present's obligation to the continued warfare of the future.

"Around the corner!" the bouncer shouted in German.

"Rifles!" ordered the refined voice of Mr. Justice Stone.

There was the sound of a cabinet unlocking, the rustling of bodies and weapons, the loading of rifles, the sotto voce of a plan formulated, related, and put into action by well-trained, obedient hands and minds.

The castle's men closed in on the short hallway.

Without even glancing at one another, Nick Carter and Annette Burden turned on their heels and ran back down the corridor, past the side door to the library, past the pennants and portraits and gleaming armor, to the window that over-looked a rolling countryside greening with spring grasses.

But directly beneath the window a wide moat dug for protection in the Middle Ages shimmered like silver sequins in the sun.

121

"Up," Annette said, pulling on the glass window probably installed in the nineteenth century.

"Better than down," Carter agreed, straining with her to open the large-paned glass.

The feet pounded into the hallway.

"There they are!" a voice shouted.

As bullets bit into the wall, Carter picked up an eighteenth-century chair and tossed it through the glass. The two agents kicked the remaining glass shards through the window as the chair splashed into the moat.

"You first!" Carter commanded, turning and firing as Annette crawled out the window and began the climb upward.

Carter's bullet tore through the center of the lead man's forehead, blasting bone, tissue, and cartilage in a waterspout that sprayed the wall and half a fifteenth-century tapestry a brilliant red. The dead man flew backward from the bullet's impact, arms outstretched, into his comrades.

The men recoiled, shocked by the pulpy head, the spuming blood, and the easy mortality. If enough time elapsed between violent deaths, the more well-trained professional often forgot the individuality of the horrifying details. Forgetfulness is man's automatic tranquilizer.

Their hesitation was all that Carter needed.

He jumped onto the ledge, dropped his gun into his pocket, and pulled himself up on the roughly cut limestone rectangles that jutted out to form the castle's outer wall. His hands bled. His feet slipped on the treacherous surface.

"Hurry!" Annette called from above on the ramparts.

He glanced down. Heads stuck out the big window, staring up. A rifle reached out.

He scrambled on.

Two bullets whizzed past his ear.

A voice screamed from below. Annette had gotten one of them.

Carter slipped and pulled himself upward, gunshots shattering his eardrums as Annette fired every time one of them stuck a head or arm out the window.

At last he reached the top and flopped over the rampart's edge, exhausted.

"No time for that," Annette said impatiently.

"What do you mean?" he panted. "You've been resting up here while I've been climbing Mount Everest!"

True to form, without a smile or any other friendly acknowledgment, she ran off around the walk that rimmed the top of the castle. At one time, an archer or bowman would have been stationed at every cut in the fortification to discourage the advances of the armies of neighboring duchies.

"Don't bother to wait for me," he called and got to his feet.

She disappeared around a corner. Behind him, shouts rang again, and he heard the rising noise of feet running with the gracelessness of an army in disarray. Heads, shoulders, and rifles appeared out of an open space behind and to his right: a wide soldiers' staircase.

"Damn!" he cursed again.

He rounded the corner, expecting to find Annette waiting, and there they'd have to make a stand. There was nowhere else to go. It would be a certain bloodbath.

But she was right again, her memory serving them both well. There was a small door.

He opened it. A narrow stairway wound darkly down. He descended eagerly, two, three stories, toward the warm aromas of Westphalian ham, spicy schnitzel, and rich strudel. His mouth salivated. He realized he was starving.

A hand grabbed his arm out of nowhere. He hadn't yet reached the kitchen.

"Carter."

Her voice. Cool, briskly collected.

"Dammit, Annette!"

"Come on," she said.

He could feel her move, pushing on something on the wall. The wall rotated.

Suddenly they were in a dining room lit only by sunshine through slatted louvers. The long table was set with antique Bavarian china, Düsseldorf sterling, and Hanover crystal. It waited suspended in time as if to serve a hunting party of nobles and aristocrats who would gather from as far away as München.

She tugged on his arm, and they stepped away from the wall. She pressed a carved panel, and the wall again rotated, returning to its proper place a narrow serving table and, above it, three stuffed grouse.

"Never did like those grouse," she muttered, striding off across the shadowy, dim room.

"Where to now, as if it did any good to ask?"

She slid the fifteen-foot-tall panel door open a crack. He peered through it, too, over her head.

"It's clear," she said, and they pushed the door open just wide enough so that they could sidle through.

They padded down another corridor that was in a different wing of the castle, obvious because of their earlier trip across the rampart fortifications. But this corridor seemed identical to the first one. Only the faces in the portraits had changed.

As they passed a window, Carter touched Annette's shoulder.

"Look over there."

A helicopter was landing on one of the rolling green lawns. The whirling blades beat the tulips, pansies, and forsythia into a froth of colors. Three men hopped out of the aircraft, heads ducked, wearing dull black jump suits, carrying M-16 rifles with telescopic sights, duffle bags slung over their backs.

"The executioners," Annette whispered.

"It won't be so easy now," Carter said. "How do we get

out of here, or don't you know?''

She strode on.

"We can't exactly walk out the front door," she said.

"Why not?" he said. "You have a better idea?"

She stopped, coldly appraising the idea.

"Bold, and they wouldn't expect it," she decided. "All right. Let's go."

He chuckled at her bright stubbornness, and the two crack agents reversed their direction and raced down the corridor toward the front of the castle. They turned corners, ran beneath chandeliers that shone with light bulbs where hand-dipped candles had once flickered, ducked into linen closets and bedrooms to avoid groups of roving sentries, passed tall ornate chairs in which no one had bothered to sit in the last hundred years, and startled young maids wearing frilly white aprons and carrying feather dusters and spray wax.

Slowly the sound of voices grew.

In a castle that was a maze of corridors and rooms, prey could hide indefinitely from even an army. But this prey—Carter and Annette—had a mission to accomplish, and they couldn't spend any more time dodging and hiding.

The executioners stood in the marble foyer, talking with Mr. Justice Stone while around them hovered first the board of directors and then the bouncer with his armed guards.

The executioners turned in different directions, nodding. One of them gestured in a sweeping move that encompassed the entire castle. Another gave a short series of barks that were orders. The guards spread out, and the three execution-ers left, heading where they had faced, walkie-talkies on their belts, M-16s ready for any action.

Carter and Annette slipped inside one more door, waited until the heavy feet passed, counted to twenty, then cracked the door, checked, and moved stealthily back into the cor-ridor.

The foyer was almost empty. Only four guards were in

sight: one on either side of the main doors, and the other two
at the back of the foyer where a wide staircase rose between
walnut pillars.

Carter flipped his stiletto into his hand. Annette watched,
nodded silently, and did the same with her own razor-sharp
knife.

They looked into each other's eyes, knowing the plan by
simple logic. They watched the guards, waiting for the right
moment when they would be looking elsewhere.

Then, silent as jungle predators, they raced the last of the
corridor, Carter easily in the lead but not by much. A light
film of sweat glistened on Annette's serious face. Her blue
eyes were steely, cold as ever.

As Carter sprinted farther ahead, she jumped the first
guard by the door. Yanked his head back to her shoulder.
Jammed the knife up under his rib cage. Blood spurted onto
the floor, and he collapsed into it just as the other guard next
to the door turned around.

Carter flipped the second guard the rest of the way, keeping him off balance.

"They're here!" one of the guards at the back of the
marble foyer shouted into his walkie-talkie.

Annette aimed, fired, and shot both men through the heart,
clean holes that erupted black with blood.

Carter snapped the neck of the guard he'd flipped. The
neck had once been thick with muscle but was now flabby
from overindulgence in food and liquor. The guard toppled
over, brain dead.

Annette was at the front door, tugging. Carter grabbed the
brass rings and pulled. Down the corridors to the right and
left, feet and shouts thundered toward them.

With Carter's strength, the doors swung open.

The two agents stared for a moment, thunderstruck.

Forty feet ahead, covering like a wall the wide drawbridge

over the shimmering moat, a company of men in camouflage fatigues marched directly toward them.

The sergeant, who bore no country's insignia on his hat or clothes, took one look at Carter and Annette, aimed his rifle, and fired. His men aimed their rifles too.

Instantly the two agents jumped aside and shoved the tall doors closed. The round of ammunition smashed a beveled floor-to-ceiling mirror at the back of the foyer.

"Shit!" Carter said, disgusted. "Up the stairs again! We've no choice!"

"Drop the lock bar across the doors!" Annette said.

"Leave it as it is!" he shouted and ran toward the stairs. "I have an idea. I want everyone inside the castle. It will make our escape easier."

"What escape?" Annette said, following him up the staircase. "Every minute our chances decrease!"

It was his turn to ignore her as they tore on breathless up the castle's four stories. Behind them in the foyer, the troops joined the castle's guards and the executioners to pursue with renewed enthusiasm. The hunters smelled blood. The two condemned agents would be trapped on the rooftop ramparts. And killed leisurely as if they were target ducks.

At the top of the castle, Carter and Annette ran out onto the empty fortifications. He gestured, leading her to the back of the castle.

"What now?" she panted, looking out over the green hills that would lead to freedom, London, and answers to the questions of what this group was and what it was doing. Stopping one leg of an octopus only slowed it. The whole entity needed to be immobilized.

He grinned at her.

"No!" she said. "You wouldn't. At least, *I* wouldn't!"

"You have an alternative?"

"I don't know how to dive!"

"Aren't you lucky," he said, picking her up. "Today's the day you get to learn."

"It's four goddamned stories!" she cried, staring down at the moat that meant freedom but also perhaps a broken limb, fractured neck, or smashed back.

"Feet first," he said. "It's safest."

The maddening noise of their pursuers topped the staircase and spread out across the ramparts.

"Then you go first. Show me."

He looked at her, acutely aware of the loss of important time.

"Promise me?" he said.

"Sure."

He set her on her feet.

Bullets whistled past them. She squatted and fired.

"I don't believe you," he decided, and knelt and fired beside her. The pursuers ducked behind ramparts and walls.

"Will you get the hell out of here?" she screamed.

He studied her. If one of them didn't do something, it'd be too late. He stepped into the rampart's cut, looked down, and gauged the distance as bullets in erratic bursts sliced through the air around him.

"I'll expect you to be thirty seconds behind me," he told her, looking back at her for an answer.

Her head was covered with blood.

She lay flat, still, unmoving in death. Her arm was crooked beneath her. The leg jutted unnaturally. A sharp pain pierced his heart.

"Annette!"

"We got her!" someone shouted triumphantly. "Now him!"

The guards, executioners, and troops swarmed over the top of the castle, their guns spraying bullets in a hail of certain death. His death.

His heart aching with loss, he leaped. He leaped not only for himself, but for Annette. Her work was as important to her as his was to himself. She cared about the world.

He hit the water with his body in perfect alignment. He sliced deep into the wet darkness, and swam underwater toward the bank. He would fulfill his assignment, resolve the problem, and stop the killers whose latest unnecessary victim had been his friend and companion Annette Burden.

THIRTEEN

From the pub across the street, Nick Carter watched a young man in a pillbox hat deliver the big gift-wrapped box and the dozen long-stemmed yellow roses to Andrea Sutton's Greek restaurant in Soho. It was six o'clock in the evening, the sun a fiery orange blaze as it settled into London's thick horizon smog.

Carter sipped his beer, the memory of Annette's death still fresh and painful. Whenever he closed his eyes, he saw her vibrance, her blond beauty, and the honest, courageous qualities that had made her a remarkably good agent. Missing her made his chest ache with a dull throb.

It had taken him three patient days to work his way out of the south German countryside, past the persistent searchers and their dogs, and reach a safe phone. And then with Hawk's speedy response of AXE equipment, he'd refitted himself and flown to London. Once there, he'd taken a taxi to Harrods in Knightsbridge, the expensive department store where he'd found the peignoir set for Andrea. Andrea would like that it had come from Harrods.

He drank his beer, giving her time to open the box, arrange the flowers, and be waiting for him. He counted on their last meeting, the memories and sex, to put her in the mood he wanted.

He'd figured out enough of what to expect from her and from the unknown organization assassinating world leaders and leaving death warrants that, this time, he'd come prepared.

No more directness. No more out-in-the-open weapons. Instead, deviousness and hidden resources.

He finished the beer and strode across the street. Empty trash cans littered the Soho sidewalks. A young punk flower vendor with purple hair called her wares. Dixieland music drifted from an American-style honky-tonk three doors away. It was still early for the dinner crowd, but late enough that after-work drinkers and the disappointed wealthy were safely, happily, on their ways to alcoholic nirvanas.

Carter passed a crowd of revelers and entered the Trojan Horse.

"Reservation, sir?"

The older man standing behind the desk had thick white hair swept back in waves, and clear polish on his fingernails that caught the lamplight in brief, bright glints.

"Nick Carter. I believe Lady Sutton is expecting me."

"Ah, yes."

The response was instant. The eyebrows shot up, impressed. Lady Sutton was obviously acting in an unusual manner.

"She said to go up. You'd know the way."

Carter nodded and walked through the dining room. He felt the curious, jealous gaze of the maître d' follow as he passed the arched alcoves displaying the small reproductions of classical statuary. At the end of the dining room he doubled back to the closed-off waiting area at the front of the restaurant near the bar, and then went through the side door that opened onto the spiral staircase.

"Nick! Darling!" she called down as he closed the door. "Come up. I've a surprise for you!"

The maître d' must have used a hidden intercom to alert Andrea that he had arrived. Carter didn't mind. It made the job simpler. He climbed the stairs.

"Champagne?" she asked, standing at the top of the landing green with hanging ferns and ivies.

She held a bottle of Mumm's and two crystal champagne flutes. She opened her arms, smiled, and turned to show off the new yellow peignoir set of lace and silk. She moved slowly, aware that it clung to her female roundness, accented her in an open, willful invitation to sex.

"The champagne later," he said gruffly.

He walked to her, picked her up, and carried her into the bedroom.

She clung to his neck, head thrown back, breathing deeply. He felt his own excitement rise, swell.

Her eyes half closed. She licked her lips.

Carter lay her on the bed. Then he took the champagne bottle and glasses from her hands as she watched him with hot eyes, and set them on the bedside table. He took a handful of the fabric of her peignoir where her breasts rose and fell. He slid the lace and silk away from the scented naked porcelain of her flesh.

She gasped. Her gray eyes flared with demanding need.

"Not yet," he said.

He took off his jacket, folded it, and draped it over a chair. He took off his shirt, folded it, and draped it over the jacket. She watched him, breathing heavily, breasts trembling. He kicked off his shoes, pulled off his socks, unzipped his pants, stepped out of them, and folded them over his shirt. She reached shaky hands toward his shorts.

He let her pull the shorts out away from his jutting maleness. She moaned, and yanked the pants down to his ankles.

"Nick, I . . ."

He pushed her back. She spread her eager legs high and open. He looked deep into the familiar gray eyes.

"Now!" she cried. "Oh, Nick. Please, *now*!"

He entered her wet heat, knowing who she was, what she'd done, and what she planned to do. Knowing and wanting her because he couldn't forget what they'd shared ten years ago. Because he remembered what he now had to do. Because the life exploding fiery between them was ricocheting the world into an uncertain, dangerous future.

"You'll join us, then?" she said two hours later as they dressed. "David knew. He knew that governments all across the world lacked the strength and foresight to take care of criminals in any meaningful, lasting way. You and David always thought alike. Oh, Nick, *do* join us and save the world!"

"I still don't know who 'us' is, and what your group is about."

"But I can't tell you yet," she said as she put on a white linen blouse and stepped into a slim, pearl-gray skirt. "First you must join us. Then you can meet my brave associates. Together we'll tell you all about it."

"I can't agree to something I know nothing about," he said as he looked in the mirror to adjust his tie. "Anyone who'd do that is a fool. And you wouldn't want a fool for a partner."

She watched over his shoulder as he straightened the tie and brushed his hair. Her chiseled face was puzzled, worried. She'd hoped he'd be quick to agree. But at least he hadn't refused.

"You told the people in David's haiku codes that I'd be investigating them," he said, looking at her in the mirror. "You ruined any chance I had of getting information. And you almost got me killed—several times—particularly by your Mr. Justice Stone in that German castle."

She nodded, aware of her guilt.

"What could I do?" she said. "I'm sorry about the Israeli

agent—I understand you were close—but I'm more sorry about my David's death. He and I . . . we shared something that you and I never had. He was a true hero. He dared to go against societal norms. We all know that what's happening in our legal systems is wrong, but David was the only one who had the courage to do something!''

Her head was high and proud, her rich brown hair thrown back over her shoulders. She looked like a queen, the widowed queen of a tragic hero. She had not loved David with the passion of her true love for Carter, but sometime in the last few years she had found a substitute—fanaticism. With fanaticism she bound herself to David in a commitment made stronger by its roots in neurosis. A fanatic was someone who redoubled his efforts after his aims were lost, and her aim to love David was now out of reach. His death had finished that.

"I came to you," Carter said, "even though I knew that you'd warned David's people. You could have had your executioners waiting to kill me. Isn't my risk great enough to show my sincerity? I won't promise you anything, but I'm willing to at least talk to your people.''

She looked at herself and Carter standing in the mirror. The gray eyes appraised them. Such a handsome couple, her expression seemed to say, so much potential . . . together they could solve the world's problems.

"Take David's place," she urged him. "Finish the work.''

"I'll talk to your associates," he said noncommittally. "That's all I can promise.''

At dawn the next day, the twin-engine Cessna left Heathrow and angled south over the English Channel and into France. Andrea was at the controls, flying as if it were a thrill second only to sex. She held her chin high, her eyes half closed. The nostrils of her upturned nose flared as if she could already smell their destination.

They continued south over Rouen, Tours, Bordeaux, and then over the Pyrenees—the high mountains of the Basques, dotted with hidden villages, isolated by stubborn independence, and colored by black berets and red cummerbunds—and into northern Spain.

After flying for miles over mountainous areas populated only by forests and game, she landed the Cessna on a blacktopped strip at the base of a long valley lined thick with trees and wildflowers.

A platoon of soldiers in camouflage fatigues ran toward them from the trees and a low brown and green shed at the end of the strip. They surrounded the plane. One of them rested his rifle over his arm and opened the door.

It was the bouncer from Werner Hall, his beefy face glowering up at Carter, wishing he had orders to kill Carter, not to ensure his safety.

"Charmed to see you again," Carter told him.

"You know each other?" Andrea said cheerfully, looking at the two men. "Already you're off to a good start," she assured Carter, smiling, then she marched briskly up steps hewn from the earth and supported by timbers.

"Is everyone here?" Carter asked.

"To meet you, yes."

He heard the pleased smile in her voice as she climbed ahead of him. Periodically she would look up the mountainside. They had mounted close to a hundred steps when he at last saw what she watched for—their destination.

"It's our aerie," she explained, waving her hand as more of the soaring structure came into view.

A natural building created out of timber, stone, and glass, its shingled roof was built in a wide vee that tilted down toward the valley as if it were a bird in pitched flight. There were three stories, each accented by sequentially wider balconies, the narrowest balcony on the lowest level. The enormous floor-to-ceiling windows on each level looked out across the valley.

The modern structure was set into the mountain, a massive building as long as a football field but as disguised by its natural materials as was a bird's nest built into the fork of two branches.

This enormous aerie would house much more than an occasional weekend meeting. And already Carter had seen signs of thorough security: wires, armed guards posted in the shadows, alarms, and what looked like in the distance gun emplacements mounted in concrete bunkers painted in camouflage colors.

The vast scope of the aerie meant money, expertise, and planning on a grand scale. David Sutton might have been ambitious, but he'd never had the connections nor the vision to activate such a mammoth undertaking.

Carter followed Andrea through a torii gate—a Japanese welcome arch—and along a gravel path lined with boulders and spring mountain flowers. The three executioners in their black jump suits stepped from the corner of the house. Wordlessly they searched Carter, took his Luger, stiletto, and gas bomb, and faded back into the dark, earth-smelling shadows from which they'd come.

Andrea watched, waiting until they'd turned. She nodded her thanks, then led Carter onto the wooden porch of the house's first level.

Behind them, the platoon spread out. Some stayed on the slope nearby, others climbed outside staircases to station themselves on the two other balconies.

Andrea turned and smiled at Carter. She straightened his tie, smoothed his lapels. Then she led him into the aerie.

FOURTEEN

Nick Carter and Lady Andrea Sutton walked through the sunny room decorated with Danish modern furniture, an old dhurrie rug, and Balinese masks hung on the natural plank walls. She led him past the fireplace with its fifteen-foot hearth and down a hallway that changed from wood-paneling to solid concrete by the time they reached the metal desk. There a guard surrounded by electronic surveillance equipment sat monitoring television cameras.

"Use the palm tester," the guard said to Andrea.

Behind him, the television screens showed sweeping views of the forest and valley, wide angles of the aerie's interior and exterior, and a group of men in camouflage uniforms sitting in a classroom where a lecturer pointed to lethal chemical compounds written on a blackboard.

Carter and Andrea walked to a steel door that showed no hinges, knob, or window. She pressed her hand against a glass plate embedded in the wall next to it.

"Each day we use a different code to enter," she explained to Carter. "Sometimes we punch in a number. Sometimes we put one of our hairs in an analyzer. Only the duty guard and his superior know the code from day to day."

The glass under her hand darkened from clear translucence

to pastel green to rich emerald. A buzzer sounded somewhere above their heads. The steel door swung open.

They walked in.

Eleven imposing men and women were seated around a long conference table that could comfortably accommodate only one more. They watched curiously, suspiciously, as Carter entered with Andrea. They were men and women in their forties, fifties, and sixties, people who gave off power and experience as casually as a beggar did his stench.

The scene reminded Carter of the one in the castle library he'd watched through the keyhole. There had been twelve people there, and now with Andrea's presence, there were twelve people here. The right number for a jury. Then the memory came to him. Of course. There had also been eleven people at the luncheon in Andrea's Greek restaurant. Again, they'd been waiting for her to complete their number . . . or perhaps waiting for David. They'd been truly shocked by David's death, and perhaps as shocked by Carter's presence upstairs in Andrea's bedroom.

Carter almost smiled.

"Monsieur Carter," said a tall, lanky man.

The Frenchman arose to stand at the end of the shiny table, his hands clasped behind him, his hawk nose jutting forward. The other members at the table looked at him with respect. To his right sat Mr. Justice Paul Stone, allowing a small smile of triumph on his aristocratic English face. The magician from Werner Hall, the same man who had asked to hire Carter's cab in Budapest, was there too.

Carter placed the others around the table from his vast memory bank of government officials. Each was high up in his nation's ranks, but not at the very top level. There were no prime ministers, presidents, or kings. Instead there were ministers of information, members of national assemblies, and even one United Nations representative, Trish Reynales from the United States. A raven-haired beauty, she watched Carter, aware that they shared the same home country, curious whether he saw the world as a more important unity, saw it her way.

His gaze moved past her and back to the French leader, Count Bayard de Montalban. At last Carter had found the true power behind the organization.

"Count Montalban," he said, nodded.

Andrea smiled, then sat in the last empty chair. It was waiting for her at the center of the table.

"Bon," the count said. 'If you will bear with us, please, Monsieur Carter. Lights."

From a door at the side of the room, a technician ran out, slipped a folding chair behind Carter, and returned to a glass-walled room. Carter sat. The count sat. A projection screen rolled down from the ceiling. The lights went out, and color filled the austere meeting room.

Photos of the attempted assassination of Pope John Paul II flashed on the screen, followed by a montage of starving children, mutilated adults missing limbs lost to carelessly produced machinery, corpses killed in international wars, civil wars, and ordinary gang street wars.

"Death and destruction," the count said somberly. "We see it all around. Human greed and ambition go unchecked in our world because no one will take the responsibility to stop the results."

Car wrecks, a sinking oil tanker, and a barren landscape where once thick grasses and healthy wildlife had flourished showed on the screen.

"The president of the country decides he needs more money for his secret account in the Grand Cayman Islands," the count said, "so he charges kickback fees from the international corporation that wants to build a factory in his nation. The president of the corporation is feeling bled by bribes, but he cannot raise prices and still remain competitive. His solution is to cut back on quality. The parts are rushed through production, and quality control doesn't have the time to weed out the defective ones. What happens?'' The count's voice rose with indignation. ''Those small, seemingly marginal parts break down. Elevators plummet. Cars go out of control. Jets crash. There is an investigation. Proclamations are made. Perhaps the corporation is even publicly embarrassed or sued. But the corporation president still rules his empire, and the president of the nation goes unnamed, unpunished, free to require more kickbacks from anyone he chooses. Meanwhile, uncounted numbers of human beings have been killed or mutilated by these two men's greed and ambition.''

As photos of war and starvation continued on the screen, the count talked on.

''You see, Monsieur Carter, we here in this room are selfless people. We believe in global justice. When Sir David first brought the concept to me, we had no idea how wide the appeal would be. We have new recruits each day, people who believe that someone—an organization or a person—*must* take charge.''

''A benevolent dictator,'' Carter said.

''That's it,'' the count said. ''Lights, please.''

There was a rustling at the table as the projector went off and the lights were turned on. The scenes on the screen had kept everyone quiet with the sense of the oppressiveness of such wide-scale, unstoppable abuse.

''We have grown tired of talk,'' the count went on, sitting stiff and straight in his chair. ''Talk is easy, cheap, and irresponsible. Action is the only means we have to stop the men and women who start wars, starve the world's people, and create the insufferable climate of immorality in which their people suffer.''

He paused as those at the table murmured agreement.

"Today's courts are a joke," he continued. "Judges have no power. Lawyers are paid to find loopholes that will free criminals. We here in this room, and men and women of conscience around the world, have taken an oath to stop this injustice."

"And what of those who disagree?" Carter said.

"They disagree for selfish ends," the English justice said. "Self-interest is what we're fighting."

"It's for the good of the ordinary man," Andrea added. "The only criminals who are ever really found guilty are the poor, and even they don't stay in prison long enough to matter."

"And you've figured out what the 'good' is that mankind need?" Carter said.

The count snorted, stood, clasped his hands again behind his back, and paced along the table.

"I know what you are getting at, young man," he told Carter in his arrogant French voice. "We do not have the right to make that decision for others. Then, pray tell, who does? God? Yes, of course, God. And it may be that God speaks through us. We would like to believe that, but we are not pretentious enough to claim it. No. Instead what we do claim, do insist, and do act on is our belief that *someone* must do *something* to stop the world's criminals. And not just the Idi Amins, but the small pickpocket, too. *All* criminal behavior. If the courts won't do it, then who better than us?"

"You're not elected," Carter said. "You can't ethically represent people who don't even know what you're doing."

"In the end, they'll be grateful," Trish Reynales, the United Nations representative said quietly.

"In the end, they'll be terrified of you," Carter argued. "You'll rule them. That is, after all, what rules people. Laws. In a democracy, those laws are created by the elected representatives of the people. But in your world, *you* are the law. What you say becomes law. And the people have no recourse.''

"We'll listen to all pleas of mercy,'' the magician said stiffly.

"The way you do now?'' Carter said. "Your victims don't even know they're condemned. How can they plead for mercy?''

"They know by their criminal acts,'' the member from Japan's department of culture said. "Each human being keeps an unconscious but very real tally of good and bad acts. We all know when we've acted criminally. Unfortunately, not everyone cares. And those are the ones condemned.''

"What about reforming the courts in each of your countries?'' Carter said. "Work to strengthen and clean them up?''

"Too long,'' said the member from Brazil.

"It's taken years for their decline,'' said Mr. Justice Stone. "Sometimes even centuries. Working through the bureaucracy to improve them could take equally as long.''

"And we would all be dead by then,'' the count said, "and what good would it do? No, Monsieur Carter. There is only one way to achieve the speed and thoroughness of a good housecleaning. And that is our way. The Rule of Justice and Standards will make the world a pleasant, safe home for us all.''

"You twelve are the Rule of Justice and Standards,'' Carter mused. "And beneath you are more juries, each in different countries, all with one or two overlapping members. Names of accused criminals are brought to the juries, papers are drawn up, investigations held. Once the investigation is over, the information is voted on by the juries, and the accused is either proclaimed innocent or guilty. And if guilty—and my guess is that the overwhelming majority are found guilty—the accused is condemned. Death warrants are issued, and the details of the execution are worked out by hired executioners.''

"That is correct," the French count said. "Very good. Perhaps Lady Sutton's glowing assessment of your skills has been accurate."

"Bayard," Andrea said, her soft gray eyes alight with the promise of the future as she addressed the count, "Nick will take David's place. They were as alike as any two men could be. He will help us triumph!"

"Not yet," Carter said, standing. He walked to the count. "You think you're improving the world. Your motive—if that is your motive, and I doubt that it is—is good. But your methods will destroy what you claim you want to save."

A deep flush rose up the count's throat. The jury members moved restlessly.

"When you create your own laws without the consent of the people you say you're taking care of," Carter went on, "you're stealing their right to choose. You're stealing their power. When you choose who will live and who will die, you're killing not just people, you're killing freedom. Freedom means not only the rights of the majority, it also means respect for and protection of the few. You say you're ridding the world of criminals. But in reality you are just as criminal as those you sentence to death."

"Nick! No!" Andrea jumped up from her chair, knocking it over. "Don't say that! Don't believe that!"

"I can't condone this kind of illegal, unethical activity," Carter insisted, his voice ringing. "If you truly believe in justice and standards, you must live impeccable lives yourselves. You can't break the laws you say you're enforcing. Putting a mock jury behind them to vote doesn't take away their illegality. You're wrong. Not only won't I join you, I'll fight you—to the death, if necessary!''

"Nick!" Andrea burst into tears, sobbing against his chest.

The count's face was mottled with rage. He stood stiffly, an old soldier who'd risen through the ranks to become a general when France was fighting the Viet Cong in Vietnam long before the United States entered that unwinnable war. He was a hero of the humiliation at Dienbienphu. After that, nothing could defeat him.

"You realize, Monsieur Carter," he said, his hawk nose jutting down at the AXE agent, "that you have condemned yourself. Bring the executioners in."

"Bayard!" Andrea said, turning to him, wringing her hands. "Please! Give him time. He'll reconsider. I know he will."

"You are a silly child sometimes, Andrea," the count said. He looked up.

The three executioners led by the bouncer from Werner Hall walked into the room. The executioners stared with interest. A new assignment. They liked their work. The bouncer, new to the field, smiled. He had a personal grudge against Carter, a man who'd made a fool of him with a female agent.

"Take him away," the count said, then he returned to the table and sat, ready to move on to new business. "Here is the death warrant. Execute him immediately."

FIFTEEN

At the back of the aerie, in a hidden courtyard hollowed out of the mountain, three different executioners led Nick Carter across paving stones toward a wall where the bullets of previous firing squads had bit deep hollows.

The door in the aerie behind them closed automatically, silencing Lady Andrea Sutton's sobs.

On the mountainside above, the tall forest waved green branches above the sheer rock from which the courtyard had been hewn. Carter turned, his back to the firing squad wall. Across from him, the aerie was a windowless wall as if whatever took place in the courtyard were already an accomplished fact, no witnesses needed for an unpleasant but necessary result of the responsibility involved.

"Only three of you?" Carter said casually. "I thought the standard was six. Sure it's legal without six?"

"No matter to us," the larger of the three executioners said in slow English. He had heavy-lidded eyes that watched the world with limited vision. "Pay's good. Rules no important." He gave a slow grin that showed uneven teeth and a malevolent disposition. A man well suited to his job.

145

"Cigarette?" the second executioner said, taking out Carter's gold cigarette case from the breast pocket of his black jump suit.

A final cigarette was still a custom among firing squad victims. Carter noted the convenience of offering the condemned man his own cigarette. Besides the expensive cigarette case, the killers had commandeered his Luger, stiletto, and gas bomb. They could afford to be magnanimous.

"Thank you," Carter said, choosing one of the monogrammed cigarettes, his initials embossed in gold on the filter.

The executioner lit it.

"Have one yourself," Carter urged the man as if he still owned the case.

The executioner looked suspiciously at Carter, not quite sure whether he was being made fun of. His brows knit with indecision.

Carter inhaled and blew a perfect smoke ring.

"Go ahead," Carter said generously. "I insist."

The hand that lashed out was the size of a catcher's mitt. The man had made up his mind.

The hand hit Carter a brutal blow across the cheek. The AXE agent's ears rang. He tasted salt. His lip was cut and bleeding.

"Just the sort of civilized behavior one would expect from a kleptomaniac baboon," Carter said, continuing to smoke.

The executioner gave a growl deep in his chest and lunged.

Panicked, his two companions grabbed him and threw him back.

"Wait!" one of them shouted. "You'll ruin everything!"

They held rifles with edgy trigger fingers on Carter. They relaxed only a moment when the aerie's door opened, then were instantly alert again. Three additional executioners dressed in official black jump suits walked out onto the courtyard's paving stones.

One was again the bouncer from East Berlin's Werner Hall, arrogant and proud of the promotion into his shiny new black clothes. But that was not what Carter's three killers were so eagerly awaiting.

In the center of the new triangle of black was Annette Burden, very much alive, a large bandage on her forehead and angry disgust on her beautiful face.

Then she saw Carter. She gasped. Her face paled in shock.

The six killers took it all in, laughing sadistically. Their joke on the two victims was a great success. With these professional executioners, killing wasn't just a job. It was a calling. And the more psychological pain they inflicted, the greater their gratification.

Annette fainted.

They laughed louder at her crumpled, white-faced shape helpless on the ground.

The momentary distraction was all the Killmaster needed.

Moving like lightning, he slammed the rock-hard flat of his hand into the throat of the closest killer, and felt the neck bones crunch.

Instantly, Annette jumped up.

The man Carter had hit collapsed, surprise embedded in the cruelty on his face.

Carter spun and kicked the belly of the second one, the man's digestive tract crushed against his spinal column. The executioner stared astonished as he keeled over in a dead faint.

Annette grabbed the shoulders of the black-clad man next to her, dropped back, and tossed him flying over her in a resounding slap against the paving stones that knocked him unconscious.

Carter rotated ten degrees, smashed his elbow up into the bouncer's chin, and heard the neck snap loose from the spine. The bouncer groaned, and urine spread a circle of shame between his legs.

All this in twenty seconds.

Stunned, the last two executioners came to life. Too close to fire, they swung their rifles like clubs.

Carter and Annette ducked, then closed in.

Waiting until the last second, Carter grabbed the arm that lashed out with the rifle, yanked down, up, and down again. The rifle fell. The man screamed as the pain of the broken arm reached his brain. Carter flattened him with a perfect punch to the chin.

"Need any help?" Carter asked Annette, grinning.

She glared at him, too busy to respond, as she twisted, dropping onto her hands. One foot shot up into a terrible blow to the last executioner's jaw. As the sound of snapping bone reverberated in the courtyard, she kicked the other foot into the man's middle, knocking the wind out of him. Blue-faced, he collapsed, sucking air.

She stood, dusting her hands.

"Sorry," she said and smiled sweetly. "Did you say something?"

Carter laughed, knelt, removed his shoe, and rotated the heel.

"Did your disposition improve in captivity?" he chuckled. He took out the coil of wire and apparatus from the heel.

"I've always had a perfect disposition," she said pleasantly, as she pulled off three of the executioners' belts and began tying the injured men immobile. "Cold and irritable. Remember, you like honest women."

"And I adore women who are also wonderful agents." He shot the wire into the stone cliff, high and to the left where it embedded in a spot that, if his estimate were correct, should put them directly over the path that led from the airstrip to the aerie. "Especially those clever enough to survive." He retrieved Wilhelmina, Hugo, and Pierre from the broken-necked executioner.

"All finished," she announced.

She picked up one of the executioner's rifles and stood back to admire the handiwork that had left the executioners trussed like pigs.

"Not yet," he told her. "Come here."

She walked to him. He put his arm around her. She looked up into his eyes and wrapped her arms around his neck.

"You weren't badly hurt?" he said, sudden tension in his voice as he remembered the torture of leaving her, her head and face bloody, her body looking dead in its awkwardness. And then, later, how he'd missed her.

"I told you that I didn't know how to dive," she said. "That moat—terrible! I don't like to do things I don't know how to do properly."

"Some excuse," he said, and kissed her.

Her lips were warm and eager as she pressed into him, her heart pounding against his.

"I thought I'd never see you again," she whispered.

"Hold tight," he said gruffly. "We'd better go now."

She tucked her head against his throat, and he fastened the harness around them and typed out on the miniature keyboard the instructions that would pull and arc the wire.

He surveyed the scene of immobilized killers, knowing there was still some time before anyone would think to check on them. He and Annette would need the time.

He pressed the "go" button, and with a whir and jerk, the advanced, miniaturized AXE machinery embedded in the cliff pulled the pair up and to the left. Slowly the mechanism increased the wire's swing. Back and forth the pair swung until, with another set of commands imprinted into the electronic equipment, the wire suddenly jettisoned out.

"Wow!" exclaimed Annette. "This is amazing!"

"Just AXE," Carter said.

The pair landed halfway down the mountainside. Quickly he undid them from the harness, and they jogged down the steps.

"Wait," he said at last.

He dashed off the path and circled. The sentry was smoking quietly in the shade of an enormous fir, bored. Good. No one had alerted them that Carter and Annette were missing. Therefore, the executioners' bodies hadn't yet been discovered.

Carter slipped up behind the guard, wrapped a steely arm around the man's neck, and jerked. Just enough pressure for unconsciousness but not enough to kill. The man would be out long enough for Carter and Annette to escape.

"Guard?" Annette asked when they resumed their jog.

"The only one I was worried about. We landed beyond most of the security equipment and sentries. There are cameras, though, and gun emplacements on the mountainside. If we keep moving, we may be all right."

At the foot of the dirt steps, they separated. She circled toward the end of the landing strip where Andrea Sutton's Cessna was tied and anchored. He saw her surprise a guard, disable him with three quick karate chops, and move on to the plane.

He continued his trek toward the semicircle of sandbags that he'd noticed as they'd flown in.

"Cigarette?" Carter said cheerfully, approaching the two young men sitting behind the machine gun.

They stared astonished at him.

"Nick Carter," he said, extending his gold cigarette case. "Remember? I came in earlier today with Lady Sutton. The count said I should take a walk around, see the place. You two boys been with the organization long?''

They were eager to make friends, but they'd been well trained, too. One of them watched Carter, an uncertain smile on his acne-pocked face, while the other picked up a sophisticated walkie-talkie.

Carter sat on the sandbag wall.

''Now, that's a new model,'' he said, indicating with his cigarette the walkie-talkie.

He leaned over as if to look. The one who'd been going to make the call hesitated. Carter smiled.

He kicked the walkie-talkie straight up into the air. Crashed a fist into the jaw of the acne-scarred youngster. Belted the other fist into the other young man's chin. Surprise and dismay clouded both guards' eyes, then they keeled over backward, mouths open, unconscious.

Carter dropped his cigarette, ground it out, and raced to the landing strip. The Cessna's motor started. Men ran out from the building at the end of the airstrip.

There were shouts from the mountainside. A rifle bullet whistled past Carter from the building. Then another and another.

The aircraft turned and bumped out toward the takeoff area, Annette watching Carter worriedly.

He tore on toward their rendezvous, the bullets hailing after.

Annette ducked. The passenger door of the Cessna popped open.

Carter leaped, grabbed a safety handle, and pulled himself in as Annette jerked the throttle. The plane shuddered and leaped ahead like a rabbit, speed suddenly its only mission.

He slammed the door.

The plane rolled on, faster and faster. Soldiers and guards ran out from the forested mountain, shouting and firing.

Expertly Annette pulled back on the throttle. The nose rose

and smoothly rode the air up toward the clouds.

The two agents breathed deeply with relief, and looked down. Angry fighters and members of the Rule of Justice and Standards stood frustrated below. Some shook their fists up at the escaping aircraft. Others ran back up the mountain to their aerie, plotting how they would defeat Carter and Annette even before the two agents had a plan.

"We've got a problem," Annette said.

"Only one?" He smiled. Nothing could be as bad as remaining in the aerie with no weapons, no help, and a firing squad with itchy fingers.

"Fuel."

He looked at the gas gauge and frowned.

"Damn."

"Can't get to London, much less Paris," she said.

"Then it has to be Madrid," he decided.

SIXTEEN

Nick Carter and Annette Burden rode in the taxi south from Madrid's airport through the clear spring twilight, listening to the rich Spanish chords of flamenco music, the enticing calls of street corner vendors, and the happy shouts of children at play.

They watched colorful Madrid pass alongside them as the citizens turned on house lights, closed businesses, walked and drove home to dinners of cold gazpacho and hot paella, innocently unaware of the murderous Rule of Justice and Standards centered in the Pyrenees only a few hundred miles north.

At twenty-five-hundred feet above sea level in Spain's central plateau, Madrid is Europe's highest capital city, boasting an invigorating mixture of old and new. From narrow, picturesque streets lined with seventeenth-century buildings to broad avenues, green promenades, and modern housing complexes, the Spanish capital since 1561 was known as a cultural and artistic center as well as a center of political upheaval caused by the often violent clash of left and right.

Carter thought about the Spanish Civil War and the evils of the forty years of Franco's fascist dictatorship. Even as recently as 1981, members of the right-wing Guardia Civil had seized the lower house of Parliament and taken hostage most of the country's leaders. But within twenty-four hours the plot collapsed because the army remained loyal to King Juan Carlos, who despite being appointed by Franco as his successor, had disbanded many organizations founded by Franco and reinstated free elections. In a nation accustomed to violence as a way of rule, Spain was turning itself around. There was hope. People really did want peace, fairness, and the rights and responsibilities of governing themselves.

At Madrid's United States embassy, Carter paid the taxi driver, and he and Annette went into the spacious building. There was a bouquet of spring roses on the receptionist's desk. She was young and freckle-faced, with the eagerness of the unsullied who saw life as a mystery to which they could and would find a happy ending.

"Ambassador Paul Hallenbeck, please," Carter said politely.

She took off her glasses and looked solemnly at the two agents.

"I'm sorry, sir," she said. "He's out of town. Perhaps I can help. Passport problems? The recommendation of a good hotel?"

"The chargé d'affaires, then. Henry Fechtman."

The young woman smiled pleasantly. She liked her job, enjoyed the friendly tourists who came in with easy problems to solve, especially those who knew the right people.

"May I tell him who's calling?"

"CRA-5."

She stared a moment, her freckled face suddenly sharp with interest. She didn't know what the code meant, but as the receptionist she'd been told to alert the ambassador or chargé d'affaires whenever it was used. She stood.

"Excuse me," she said.

She bustled off, her heels clicking on the marble floor with importance. The message was too significant—and too exciting—to be given over the telephone.

She came back quickly and sat at her desk.

"He'll be right out," she said, busying herself with file folders, sneaking curious sidelong looks at the man and woman in the reception area.

Soon Henry Fechtman walked out toward the two agents, a hand extended in greeting, a puzzled smile on his face.

"Hello, Mr. . . . ?" he said.

He was a short, red-faced man with a bull neck and a flat, boxer's belly. He wore an open-necked pale blue shirt tucked neatly into tan slacks belted tightly at the waist to show his fine physique.

"Mr. Fechtman," Carter said, shaking the hand. "Mind if we step into your office?"

"Of course not. Excellent idea."

The chargé d'affaires shot a sweeping gaze of approval at Annette, flexed his shoulder muscles unconsciously, and led them down a short hallway to his cheerfully lit office.

"Have a seat," he offered, indicating the two leather-covered chairs. "Sorry. I was about to take off. Caught me just in time."

He closed the blinds on the window through which the nighttime city's lights sparkled. Now they couldn't see out, but no one could see in either. The two agents sat down. Annette sighed, and held her forehead a moment in relief.

"What's this all about?" Fechtman asked, looking from one to the other. "Which one of you is CRA-5?"

"I am," Carter said. "I need your identification. A precaution. You understand."

Fechtman folded his hands on top of his desk, which was ornately carved in the Spanish way. Hanging behind him on the white wall were two original Goya etchings. Fechtman had taste, and the good luck to be placed in an embassy where office furnishings had high priority. The chargé d'affaires—who was also a secret CIA man—thought for a moment, then spoke.

"Certainly, Mr. Carter," he said. "CRA-98. Does that help?"

Carter nodded. The ultrasecret CIA number was the correct one for Fechtman, a number Ambassador Hallenbeck would be the only other person at the embassy to know. The CIA was a cautious, highly security-conscious agency. No one was told any more than was absolutely necessary.

"We've come to ask for your help," Carter said, and he told the story of what he and Annette Burden had discovered about the secret, chilling Rule of Justice and Standards league.

As he and Annette related the tale and the scope of the series of assassinations of high government officials, Fechtman's ruddy face turned heavy with seriousness. When Carter had finished, he slapped an angry hand onto his desk top.

"Appalling!" he said, picking up the phone and dialing. "I'm calling a friend over at the palace. We'll send the army to rout out their hideout immediately. They must be stopped!"

He spoke for ten minutes, shunted from friend to official and then to higher officials. At last, mopping his brow with a large white handkerchief, he hung up. He smiled.

"As you heard," he said, allowing a small note of triumph into his voice, "it's taken care of on this end. But for the larger problem, the international scope of these assassinations, perhaps you'd better contact Hawk?"

"Of course," Annette said, "and I must call my people."

For a moment the chargé d'affaires looked startled, then nodded.

"Naturally."

There was a note of discouragement in Hawk's voice when he first answered from far-off Washington, then excitement as he recognized Carter's voice.

"Where the hell have you been, N3?" he growled.

As Carter once more began the tale, he heard the click of Hawk's butane lighter and the long, drawn-out, satisfying inhalation of the first puff of a new cigar. Hawk had settled in, and Carter continued the story.

"CRA-98, Fechtman, ODF," Carter finished, "has taken care of seeing that the hideout in the Pyrenees is disabled. He requests that you notify all governments of the Rule of Justice and Standards scheme, and says more detailed information will be forthcoming with names and addresses of league members."

There was a pause at the other end of the line. Hawk was puffing furiously.

"ODF," Hawk said. "You're sure?"

"Positive." Carter smiled at Fechtman, who was watching him curiously.

"You'll activate the location searcher?" Hawk said.

"Already did that this morning. Everything seems to be under control. We can thank Fechtman. Moves swiftly and efficiently. Perhaps you'd like to dictate a commendation for his CIA file, sir."

Hawk cleared his throat in the distance.

"Get back to me soon," the AXE chief said gruffly. "I'll be ready. You've done fine work. And . . . take care of yourself, N3. You're in a hornet's nest for sure. I've grown rather fond of you."

There was silence on both ends of the line after the unaccustomed intimacy.

"Thank you, sir," Carter said at last.

"Happy hunting," Hawk said, once again his crusty self.

Smiling, Carter hung up the phone.

A buzzer on the desk sounded. Fechtman leaned over and pressed the toggle.

"Yes?" he said.

"Your uncle and his friends are here," the receptionist announced.

"Send them in," Fechtman said, turning off the intercom.

Now he, too, smiled.

"Uncle?" Annette said, puzzled. "I thought you were leaving for home."

"The great Killmaster," Fechtman chuckled nastily, "and his latest sidekick, this one an empty-headed Israeli bombshell."

Annette reared up, grabbing for Carter's Luger. She'd had to leave her rifle in the Cessna. A rifle was too difficult to explain to a cabbie.

"Forget it," Fechtman said, sitting square behind his desk. "I've had an M-16 on you from the beginning. Drop the weapons, Killmaster—the little gas bomb too—or I'll kill you both. Your woman first."

"The count has arrived," Carter told Annette, placing his Luger carefully on the desk, then adding the stiletto and gas bomb.

"Well, Killmaster," Fechtman said, impressed. "Perhaps you're as good as you're advertised to be."

"How did you guess?" Annette asked Carter.

"Regular CIA wouldn't know my name," he told Annette. "How did he know that, and about AXE and Hawk, if he weren't warned and prepared beforehand by the count's people?

"Ah, Monsieur Carter," Count Montalban said suavely as he walked into the chargé d'affaire's office accompanied by eight executioners. "How lovely to meet again. Most unusual circumstances, but . . ." He turned to Fechtman. "Henry, the plan goes?"

"Smooth as silk, sir," Fechtman said. "Carter gave the information to the AXE head Hawk as you suggested. He'll be kept busy informing governments and treading water, waiting for us to get back to him with names and addresses."

"Your telephone call to the palace was phony!" Annette accused Fechtman. "You made it all up!"

He laughed.

"Of course. Hollywood didn't think I had any talent, but the CIA always has use for a man with imagination."

"And the Rule of Justice and Standards," Carter added.

"We're delighted to have Henry's professional services," the count said, gesturing the group toward the door. "Come. It's time."

"But how did you know to find us here?" Annette wondered.

One of the black-suited executioners prodded her with his rifle as she stood stubbornly waiting for an answer. She turned and shot an icy glare at the man. The count, a gentleman of the old school, raised a hand, and the executioner backed off.

"Preparations, my dear," the count explained. "We had similar plans at all the embassies, but of course the likelihood was that you'd come here. Only enough gas for Madrid. A war is won not just on an army's stomach, but also on its close attention to details. Now we really must go."

The count nodded to the executioners, and they milled out, escorting their prize—the two agents—tightly surrounded by guns and bodies. The group walked down the short corridor to the reception room, past the receptionist who was tied and gagged to her office chair, her unsullied face once so excited by life now pale with fear, and past twenty other embassy personnel—cooks, gardeners, file clerks, secretaries, maids, handymen—who were tied similarly to chairs in the reception area.

"Is that all of them?" the count asked a camouflage-outfitted soldier who approached and saluted smartly.

"Yes, sir!" the man said.

"Everything ready?" the count went on, leaning down to peer over his jutting hawk nose at the soldier who stood stiff at attention.

"Yes, sir!"

"Very good," the count said. "Let's go."

Now two dozen strong, the group moved out the front doors and down the path to the sidewalk where long black limousines waited. Soldiers and executioners climbed into the string of cars. The count gestured to Annette and Carter to get in the second limousine, then to three of the soldiers. He climbed in last. The caravan moved off.

When they'd driven about a block, the explosion went off.

The ground rocked. The blast thundered through the air. People ran out on the sidewalks, and the limousines sped ahead.

"The embassy," Carter said, his stomach turning over. He thought of the freckle-faced secretary, the innocent office personnel. Murdered.

"You bastard!" Annette cried, her cool blue eyes flashing like sapphires with the horror.

The count nodded.

"They were all corrupt anyway," he explained.

SEVENTEEN

The group changed jets twice during the night, and on the third jet the entire jury from the Pyrenees aerie joined them. About thirty jury members from the various levels sat in the first class section, smoking, talking quietly, some gazing out the windows as morning showed Africa's deserts and savannahs shimmering gold, spaced intermittently by the dark green foliage of dense overgrown jungles.

In tourist class behind, about fifty executioners and soldiers, who were training to be executioners themselves, slept or played solemn-faced poker. The executioners played only with other executioners, and the soldiers, the decision made for them, also played only with one another. Rank was important among all forms of life. The men seldom talked, the intensity of winning more important than any momentary human need to communicate.

Nick Carter and Annette Burden sat at the back of the first class section, two executioners across the aisle guarding them. Count Montalban had been explicit about which seat each of the first class passengers was to sit in, even the prisoners, and his subordinates had deferred without complaint but with strained smiles to his wishes.

The aircraft was passing over Lake Rudolph in north

Kenya's arid plain when the count roused himself to walk up and down the aisle, stopping to smile and chat, attending to the politics of leadership.

Lady Andrea Sutton sat next to Mr. Justice Paul Stone, her chin high as she defied Carter's rejection. But occasionally the soft gray eyes darted back, unable to stop themselves, taking in the bitter sight of Annette and Carter sitting hand in hand. She would flinch, jerking her gaze away, and return to the business of being a leader of the world's only hope for civilization—the Rule of Justice and Standards. She'd made an uncomfortable compromise with herself.

"But we must be very careful, *mon vieux*," the count was saying to the magician whom Carter had at last placed as a great-grandson of Kaiser Wilhelm. "Only the best people. Your nominee does not have the background, the . . . if you will forgive me . . . the pedigree. One of the attitudes wrong in the modern world is that class makes no difference. Nonsense! A man with the proper rearing, the right schools, a cultivated taste for literature, art, learning—that man was born to lead. He has bred into him the ability not only to make decisions, but to make the *right* ones."

"And who, dear Count," said the member from Japan, "constitutes the 'best' people?"

The jury members watched uneasily as the arrogant count smiled patronizingly down at the Japanese minister of cultural affairs.

"Ah! Thought you would catch me, did you, Totura? The old man is not off his bonnet yet. There is plenty of room for the likes of you. Women, too. Have to have them these days. I know you Japanese do not like them either, what with their caterwauling about property and inheritance rights, but times have changed."

The first class passengers shifted unhappily. The soldiers and executioners in the tourist compartment and the two executioners guarding Carter and Annette appeared uninterested and unmoved.

"But they will not run things. No," the count went on, stroking his chin thoughtfully. "Can't go too far. History is a great teacher, and what we have learned is that white Europeans of the old aristocracy are the ones who conquered the world. You people had your chance when you bombed Pearl Harbor, but you just did not have the necessary vision and persistence. You could have—and should have—won the war right there."

A ruddy flush spread across the Japanese minister's cheeks. He knotted his hands into fists, then glanced uneasily at the executioners. They stared right through him. The other league members looked at the executioners too, then turned their backs as if they wished the whole conversation—and the hints it gave about the megalomaniac count—would evaporate.

"Now take dear Andrea," the count said, strolling up the jet's aisle. "A man with sex appeal comes along, and she's a whimpering weakling." He patted her shoulder. She cringed away from the hand, but he didn't notice. "She does not mean to be, of course. Can't help herself. That is the difference between a man and a woman. Strength of character."

He laughed heartily. Several of the jury members joined him.

Beside Carter, Annette moved restlessly. He squeezed her hand, warning her to control her anger.

"We are interested in new members at any time," the count continued as he returned to his seat. "But not all of them can expect to be on the juries. We must be careful, very careful, of our choices. I will seriously consider all nominations, but you must not be surprised when I veto a few. After all, the whole concept is quality of life. And who better knows that than those who've lived the best lives?"

The count retired to sit alone in regal splendor in his seat.

A sigh of relief wavered through the first class compartment. The executioners and soldiers remained unmoved. They had been paid to be loyal only to the count. An enormous family fortune that could afford many expensive salaries was still worth something.

Some of the various jury members slumped unhappily in their seats, others stared stonily ahead, while several slipped into the contentment of knowing they were right about the count and life.

But some had been surprised and offended by the count's bigotries. Although powerful and independent in their own countries, here they were subservient to the count and his staff. To attack the count was the same as attacking the executioners. The well-trained, ruthless, black-suited executioners were enemies no one wanted. They took too much pleasure in their work. And so the offended jury members remained silent about their objections.

The cabin quieted. The soft slap of playing cards and called poker bets echoed from the back. The count turned on the intercom system of piped-in music. He chose Chopin's Second Sonata, leaned back, and closed his eyes.

Annette watched him, irritation and worry growing on her finely modeled face.

"Now what do we do?" she whispered to Carter. "No weapons. We can't escape while we're in the air. If you knew what was going on at the embassy, why didn't you let me know? We could've escaped!"

"I alerted Hawk," Carter explained in a hushed voice. "That was my first priority."

"But he has wrong information! He thinks everything's under control!"

"He knows Henry Fechtman was ODF."

"ODF? I remember your using the acronym when you

talked to him, but I assumed it was part of the CIA code.''

"It's AXE code for 'operative disfunctional,'" he said, smiling that the deception had worked not only with Annette, but apparently with Fechtman, too. "So he knows something was wrong about Fechtman, and that I'd activated my location searcher. AXE people are tracking us now, and have been since this morning. That means that they know where the aerie is. Hawk will send a team to observe, and when he figures out that the Spanish government has done nothing about it, he'll notify them."

She looked at him with her large blue eyes. She shook her head, the blond curls bouncing.

"I didn't see any of that," she said, her low voice dismayed. "I must be losing my touch."

"Never your touch." He grinned at her. "You're used to giving the orders. When you're in charge, you know more than everyone else . . . or you'll fail."

"But . . . but . . ." The blue eyes snapped as thoughts clicked into place. "We're still in terrible danger. And the count . . . he's frightened his people into subservience. He can have us—or any of them—executed instantly. And go on unstopped with his vigilante plans. His success has already led to twenty successful assassinations all around the world."

"Unfortunately true," Carter agreed. "That's why we didn't escape at the embassy when we had the chance. We've got to stop him now. No one else can. This job's up to us."

The timbered fort was set high on stilts on the dry land, surrounded by thornbush, acacias, and baobab trees that reached awkward arms to the Kenyan sun. Carter knew they were in south Kenya because of the vegetation, but also because in the distance the slopes of Tanzania's distinctive Mount Kilimanjaro rose to a majestic snowy peak.

The jet had landed on a private strip on the flat land. Waiting along the landing strip had been a string of Jeeps that carried the passengers to the fort. Warm bath water, fluffy white towels, and stiff drinks were waiting there, the native servants fetching and carrying as the thirty members of the various juries and the fifty executioners and soldiers made requests that were given as orders. But the natives didn't complain. Good pay and infrequent contact made even a boor palatable.

Carter and Annette's room was simple, a grass mat for a bed, bars on the window, and three locks on the outside of the door. A native brought two simple, smocklike garments, and the count entered the room, four executioners immediately behind with their rifles.

"We must resolve one last problem, Killmaster," the count said, peering down over his nose like a schoolmaster instructing a wayward, belligerent student. "No more hidden weapons. No magic wires that shoot into cliffs to help you escape. The only way you will leave here is in a coffin—or by your own volition if I decide to trust you enough to allow you to join my cause."

"I thought we'd settled that issue," Carter said.

The count walked over to the sleeping mat and kicked it. Dust from the straw danced in the sunlight.

"Whereas your escape would anger most opponents, it only increased my respect—and my curiosity—about you," the count said. "I have decided to allow you to live for the time being, and to show my good faith, to allow Mademoiselle Burden to live also. We have here a moment-ous event." He swung his arm in a grandiose gesture that took in the entire compound. "Our first international meet-ing. Our success has been great enough that we have proved to ourselves and to the world that our cause deserves to go on. Now we must complete our plans, authorize them, and move quickly with our revolution in justice. You will stay with us, hear the plans, choose once more. If again you will not join, then you must die. Simple, n'est-ce pas?''

He picked up the garments, nodded to the natives who scuttled out of the room, and tossed the clothing to Carter and Annette.

''Put these on. My men will take your clothes away. And to make certain you hide no more of your deceptive weapons, my men will watch.''

Annette stiffened. The count shrugged.

''In some cases,'' he told her, ''gallantry is indeed dead.''

He smiled, nodded, and marched out through the door.

''Do it,'' one of the executioners said. His forehead was low and his eyes set close together. ''Now.''

''Absolutely not,'' Annette declared.

The executioner raised his rifle and aimed it at her.

''I have orders to kill you if you refuse,'' he said, smiling cruelly. ''Please refuse.''

His two companions snickered, watching with interest, their rifles, too, raised.

''No!''

She flung the shift across the room, then lunged.

Carter grabbed her around the waist and held her struggling to him.

''You kill her,'' he said to the executioners, ''and the count will be disappointed. In you, not in her or me.''

''He said—''

''But what will he say if you actually do it?'' Carter asked reasonably. ''How can she join if she's dead?''

Unhappy, the three men looked at one another. The count was very important to them. They didn't want to lose his favor, or the regular pay. But they were professionals, supposed to make their captives do what they were told.

''Let her stand behind me,'' Carter said. ''She'll have

privacy, and you'll get what you want—the clothes.''

Once more the three killers checked each others' reactions.
At last the lead one nodded.

''Make it quick,'' he said.

''Annette?'' Carter said.

She'd stopped her wriggling and nodded angrily, her curls
bouncing.

He released her. The executioner tossed the shift back at
her. She caught it and stalked behind Carter. He could feel
the heat of her rage. Still he undressed, hearing her undress
behind him. He put on the garment, and she walked to his
side, also dressed in the simple cotton shift.

Silently relieved, the executioners picked up the clothes
and left.

''Now what do we do?'' she asked, anger hiding the same
obvious fear that Carter felt. ''They've taken everything!
We'll never stop the count! Never get out of here alive!''

EIGHTEEN

All through the day, the spring sun beat onto the wood-shingled roof, warming the room. Nick Carter and Annette Burden watched sunbeams dance in the shafts of sunlight through the barred window. They listened to the heavy-booted Rule of Justice and Standards soldiers and execution-ers walk their beats around the balcony that circled the Kenyan fort.

The two agents sat apart on the floor as they had in the Hessian house in Lübeck, West Germany, not touching. They were separated by a wall of uncertainty, and a strong feeling of their impending deaths.

"I don't remember much," Annette said, once more try-ing to explain her life to herself. "Sometimes I think I walk backward into the future, my eyes firmly fixed on the past. I can't shake what happened before. It's part of me, like my skin. In Jerusalem, there are bombings and hatred, but also there's much tolerance and love. Someone once said that organized religion was responsible for more death than any disease or war. If that were true, then Jerusalem is the place to go to see how that doesn't have to be. Different cultures and religions walk shoulder to shoulder down the old and new streets despite the constant threats and killings. To stand up against that, day after day, year after year, without being tainted by it shows remarkable courage. And that there are other choices.''

''You came from a strongly religious background?'' Carter asked.

''Not orthodox, but reform. My father read the Torah. My mother lit the candles every Friday night. I'd watch the flames flicker and wonder that all the rest of the world weren't as mesmerized as I was by the brightness of the light.'' She crossed her legs and leaned back on her elbows on the straw mat. ''But when they died, the flames weren't the same any longer. Dull somehow. Uninteresting. Finally, boring. By the time I arrived in Israel, I had a chip on my shoulder. Angry about life, like you said. I was furious. Nothing mattered anymore.'' She laughed at the painful memory and shook her head. ''Working on a kibbutz rearranged my priorities. We needed each other there. Need mattered. And, finally, life mattered again. Everyone was everyone else's family. Somewhere in there I learned to distance myself from the anger. To not care so much about it anymore. I suppose that's why I seem cold to people. But I'm not, really. Just careful. When I love, I love deeply, but the anger is still there. Always will be, I suppose. But I've learned to live with it. It doesn't control me anymore.''

''Israel is lucky to have you,'' Carter said quietly. ''Any country would be. The biggest disease our world has is lack of commitment. People don't care enough to take risks, stand up, say what's right or wrong. In that, the count is correct. And that's why he attracts followers. It's healthy for people to get mad about injustice—just as you did about the injustice of your parents' death. What's not healthy is staying angry. When people do, after a while, as you discovered, nothing else matters but the rage. We don't have enough people who can make healthy commitments, take healthy risks. Instead we have neurotics whose anger becomes more important to them than the injustices that caused it.''

''Is that where Lady Sutton fits in?'' Annette said, glancing sidelong at him.

Carter cleared his throat.

''It's not easy in her case,'' he said slowly. ''It's a combination. A love affair that didn't go the way she wanted. Marriage to a man she didn't love. Leaving the service. Guilt about both. And trying to recapture herself by resurrecting the reasons she became an agent in the first place—her outrage at injustice.''

''You're saying she went off the deep end,'' Annette said.

''Something like that.''

''Any of us could.''

''We have different tolerance levels, but, yes,'' he said, ''theoretically we all have our snapping points. You didn't break. You found a channel for your anger and, by working with it, a way to control it. Sometime on the kibbutz, you gave up rage as the most significant thing in your life.''

She smiled, a slow, deep smile. He felt the tingle of her female call across the empty inches between them.

''Lady Sutton's love affair was with another agent,'' she deduced.

''Yes,'' he said, uncomfortable.

She rolled onto her side and propped her head on her hand, elbow on the floor. She looked quizzically at him.

''You,'' she said.

''Guilty,'' he said. ''Do you mind?''

''I'm thinking about it.''

''Keep smiling while you're thinking.''

''I'm not ready to let you off the hook so easily.''

She studied him, her face a mask of disinterest.

''What if I tell you I'm jealous?'' she said.

''I won't lie to you,'' he said, ''or try to convince you there was nothing between her and me. There was a lot. Once. Long ago.''

Her eyes blazed.

''And now?'' she asked.

Her fire and passion spread out to him, inviting, demanding. He was her man, and she wouldn't let him go.

He caught his breath, and cradled her chin. She shivered, staring boldly at him. He looked into her eyes, and the blueness deepened into the fathomless color of the ocean's.

''Forget about her,'' she said, her lips moving toward him.

''A man could drown in your eyes,'' he said.

She kissed him, soft, pliable lips that pulled, pulled him into her.

His heat spread, then the need, its demands. He crushed her to him.

There were boots on the balcony. The steps stopped at their door.

She stiffened. The door opened.

Disgust spread across the evil face of the executioner as he took in the scene of the two on the floor.

''The count says come,'' he said, his rifle resting across his arm. ''Now.''

Carter and Annette exchanged a look of frustration, but also acknowledgment. At last the time had arrived for the issue of the Rule of Justice and Standards to be settled. It meant either their deaths, or the resolution of the insidious problem that threatened the foundations of the civilized world.

Carter and Annette sat in the back of the large meeting room. Glass windows that overlooked the dry plain were behind them. Their seats faced a sea of chairs, a wall of maps, and a podium behind which Count Montalban stood in haughty grandeur as the room filled with members of his various juries.

During the day, three more jets had arrived with members from Africa, North and South America, and Australia. There was seating for sixty in the spacious, skylighted area, plus there were the soldiers who rimmed the room, and the executioners who prowled restlessly along the outside balcony and inside halls. The count, the executioners, and the soldiers were the only people with weapons.

Occasionally Carter glanced over his shoulder through the windows and saw in the distance glimpses of gnu, lions, prowling hyenas, and lumbering elephants. As the count sipped a glass of water and the meeting hall filled to capacity, all talk stopped.

The ground shook with a rolling thunder that grew louder and louder.

Some of the members looked nervously around. Others laughed, shouting in the ears of the worried ones. They stood at the windows, gaping. A herd of antelope thundered toward the Kenyan fort, clouds of dust swirling gray and brown tornadoes in the crystal air.

The fort's floor and walls shook as thousands of the beasts passed under the structure that had been built high to accommodate even the spindly-legged, long-necked giraffe in flight. For fifteen minutes the men and women of the league stood there, watching, mesmerized by nature's strength and glory.

Carter studied the viewers as the last of the antelope galloped below. He reminded himself that the well-dressed, wealthy, powerful members were on a collision course with thousands of years of civilization, trying to reduce law to the level of animal instincts.

Annette looked at him.

"Will Hawk come?" she whispered. "Will he send troops?"

Carter smiled at her.

"I've already pressed the switch in the location searcher." He pointed to his side where the small electronic device was embedded beneath his skin. "But there's no way to determine when he'll arrive."

"Or if," she said, her face pale with worry.

The members of the Rule sat quietly in their seats, drinking coffee, as various reports were made from around the world. Formal requests were made for executioners to serve death warrants in Los Angeles, Johannesburg, Tripoli, Moscow, and Buenos Aires.

All were approved without discussion of the cases involved. Once the individual juries had rendered their verdicts, their decisions were accepted by the count.

"And now for the reason for this momentous meeting," the count said at last, speaking in English, the international language of the members.

The men and women watched him expectantly, their respect enormous. Only a few—some of those who rode on the jet with him earlier that day—seemed worried and uneasy. Carter was counting on them. He intended to make them his secret weapon.

"After careful consideration," the count said, and he flipped down a see-through plastic overlay with red painted numbers to cover the map of Europe and Asia, "we have determined there is one assured means of changing the direction of the world from criminal chaos to civilized rule."

He walked to the next map and turned down another overlay with red numbers. The members murmured, some curious, a few concerned. He dropped overlays over the rest of the maps that covered the world's land masses. All had red numbers that seemed to cluster on the capitals and major cities.

"The world is overrun with crime," the count said, gesturing at the maps. "We would not be here if life were otherwise. From the man who steals a loaf of bread to the president of a country who steals a corporation by nationalizing it, our globe is stained by massive corruption. But unlike the man in the street whose crime affects only a few, corrupt government leaders affect all of us. Therefore, our plan begins at the top."

Audience members nodded. Accustomed to a certain amount of power themselves, they understood its ramifications.

"Part of the problems of leadership," the count continued reasonably, "is the lack of training. A farm boy with muscle, wile, and luck can fight his way to the top of a dictatorship. What kind of training is that to lead a nation? A woman who spends her life following her husband from job to job, sewing, caring for her children, giving parties, becomes the head of her country because her popular father dies and names her his successor. How can she sensibly lead any country?"

Murmurs grew in the audience. A scattered few clapped with approval. The count inclined his head, pleased.

"Therefore," he said, "our responsibility is clear. We must replace the untrained and the corrupt. We must help the governments of the world begin afresh!"

This time more people applauded, and as the applause continued, even more joined. The faces of those clapping beamed, lit by an inner fire of enraged righteousness that fed hungrily on the count's words. Somewhere deep inside, every man dreamed of being a savior, of buying immortality.

Carter stood up.

"Count Montalban," he said.

The count's eyes narrowed.

"There will be time for questions later," he said, his words clipped as if he were dismissing a servant . . . or a slave.

"Not a question, an observation," Carter said. "You're obviously planning to assassinate the top world leaders."

Several members in the audience gasped, turning to stare at Carter.

"How do you plan to keep their citizens in line?" Carter asked. "Will you take over their armed forces as well?"

Angry muttering swept through the room. Some were upset by the thought that the count would conceive such horrible acts. But the majority were unhappy that Carter had interrupted, stolen the count's glory in setting forth his plan.

"Now, now," the count soothed his followers, "Monsieur Carter has raised some interesting points." A fine sweat covered his face. His hands trembled as he gestured toward the AXE agent at the back of the room. "He is an astute man, not always ethically correct, but I bow to his quick grasp of the situation. It is our responsibility to put *true* leaders in charge of the world's nations. No more helter-skelter, mish-mash of semiliterate, untrained, ambitious demigods. It is all perfectly legal. The justice papers were drawn, and I myself conducted the investigations."

He paused significantly, lengthening the moment of his audience's complete attention. He reveled in his power. His followers watched raptly, some frozen-faced with horrified disbelief.

"I have death warrants on twenty world leaders," he went on. "Eventually we will be forced to execute more. The chronology and location of the deaths is listed on the maps in the order of importance. Note carefully. And, of course, Monsieur Carter is correct. We will have to execute the leaders of their military machines and take them over, too. They are all corrupt anyway."

"And what of your leaders?" Carter asked. "Who will you choose to lead the nations?"

"Ah, excellent thinking," the count said. "We will have white European males, of course, particularly those with aristocratic backgrounds. Certainly none without the approved schooling in the right institutions and military branches. Joined together, we will direct the earth along the path of truth! We will kill *all* heads of *all* governments, and most of their associates, except those that are with us! It will be a bright day that dawns over the empire of the Rule of Justice and Standards!"

His voice rang in the room, a fist shaking above his head. The first ruler of the world.

"Racist!" Carter shouted. "Sexist! Bigot!"

At Carter's brave words, some of the followers jumped to their feet. Many were of different races, and many were women. But there were also an equal number of the white European males that the count deemed to be his loyal supporters and logical successors on their feet protesting, too. The soldiers and executioners came to attention. Those loyal to the count shouted out their support. The executioner behind Carter's chair with the evil face grabbed Carter's arms and yanked them cruelly back.

"Death to all who defy me!" the count yelled in return, his hawk nose lifted high. He no longer bothered with the aristocratic, compassionate veneer. His face glowed with the relief of abandoning it. "I will kill you all! All! If you defy me!"

It was the last, too-heavy straw. As Carter hoped, the chaos erupted into pandemonium. Small pistols seemed to appear from nowhere. The count's powerful subordinates hadn't risen high in their own countries because they were fools. Some of them wore concealed arms.

Shots ricocheted through the room. Shouts echoed.

"Stop them!" the count bellowed, ducking behind the podium.

Carter jabbed an elbow back. Annette smashed a fist into the executioner's jaw. The executioner fell heavily across the chair.

Once free, Carter whirled, kicking a soldier in the stomach. The man collapsed, gasping.

Carter grabbed Annette's hand.

"Let's get out of here!"

NINETEEN

Shock and savagery were two key survival techniques in the free-for-all of any pandemonium. Shock at first caused hesitation. Some of the brawlers used it to their advantage, punching, stripping weapons, shooting, while their slower-reacting companions stood in a daze, confused.

Count Montalban jumped up behind the podium from where he'd ducked.

"Give up!" he shouted to the insurgents. "Give up at once and you can rejoin our crusade of justice!"

Savagery took over as the executioners and soldiers protected their leader. Coldly they picked targets among the insurgents and shot them dead while the count watched warily, shouting instructions and encouragement, ducking when one of his opponents turned on him.

Those objecting to the count's plan either ran terrified from the room or squatted behind chairs and tables, trying to protect themselves while picking off the count's men with smaller-powered handguns that in the end killed just as dead as did the executioners' big rifles.

Mr. Justice Paul Stone tossed Lady Andrea Sutton a rifle he stole from the corpse of an executioner.

The two key English members of the Rule of Justice and

Standard exchanged a look of painful disillusionment, and fired back at their former friends who would now kill them. Their insurgent group was badly outnumbered, and as the battle continued in spurts of stealth and gunfire, the count at last took out his own ivory-handled pistols.

"Damn you all!" he shouted. "The faithless! The stupid and willful! I have a plan that will save us all. *I* will rule the world!"

He shot one man in the heart as he raised up to fire at a soldier.

He killed a woman who fought next to Andrea with a bullet that blasted through an ear and blew half her head away.

Then he fell behind the podium again as the remaining insurgents turned to fire on him.

The vast majority of the members still in the hall were the count's supporters, but because of the confusion they weren't always easy to distinguish from his objectors.

Leading a group of about twenty, the chargé d'affaires from the Madrid embassy, Henry Fechtman, tried to join the lines of the executioners and soldiers. But the count's men shot the group as if they were attacking instead. Fechtman fell and crawled away, a wound in his shoulder, blood trickling between the fingers of the hand that held it.

Close to one of the room's four doors was the magician from the East German cabaret, the great-grandson of Kaiser Wilhelm. He and many others slipped out and escaped into the halls. The rest of the supporters, farther from the doors, lay flat on the floor, arms over their heads, quaking, trying to stay alive until the soldiers and executioners killed off the opponents.

Again the count rose behind the podium, his ivory-handled pistols shaking.

"Fools!" he cried. "Idiots! You'll die! I condemn every one of you to death!"

As gunfire continued to ring in the room, and the smell of cordite, fear, and retribution rose, Nick Carter snatched the rifle of the executioner whom Annette Burden had knocked out.

She grabbed a rifle from a dead soldier whose hands had clamped like locks onto it in his death throes.

The row of the count's kneeling, shooting men stretched toward the doors on either side.

"Which way?" Annette said.

Carter forged ahead, slamming the rifle butt down on the back of the head of the closest soldier. The man tumbled forward, blood streaming from the wound.

The men around the downed man looked up, suddenly aware a distant bullet had not gotten their comrade.

Carter kicked the belly of the closest one. The man doubled over, green-faced, falling headfirst to the floor.

Annette understood quickly what Carter was doing.

She dropped to her hands, and with lightning-quick kicks of her feet, widened the circle around them. Four of her victims dropped unconscious to the floor.

With an angry bellow, an executioner swung his rifle up to aim directly between Carter's eyes.

Carter charged him, lashing the rifle from the man's hands, and barreled into him, head down. The head pinioned the man, making him into a protective wall for Carter and Annette.

Helpless, arms flailing, the man rushed backward to the door, Carter propelling him. Annette clung close behind Carter, shooting anyone who turned to fire on them.

"That's a new one, Killmaster!" Annette said breathlessly as she slammed the balcony door safely behind them.

Carter grinned and stood up.

The executioner stumbled backward, arms still flailing, now wild-eyed with rage and fear. Too eager to escape, he fell backward over the rail into the dust of the Kenyan plain.

"Interesting response," Carter said, peering down over the side as the man stood and shook a fist up at the two agents.

"What now?" Annette said, looking around.

Two corpses dead from chest wounds lay spread-eagled in the bright sunshine on the balcony's timbered floor.

Carter stretched, checking back through the glass window to the main room. Spatterings of gunfire continued. The soldiers and executioners were closing in on the insurgents.

There were about fifteen of the insurgents left, shooting from behind tables and chairs. Most of the count's supporters had escaped now, only a few lying still as corpses to avoid that fate.

There were close to fifty of the count's men left fighting in the big meeting hall, and with the count watching behind the podium, urging his men on, helping with a few well-placed bullets, the fifteen defiant men and women wouldn't live long.

"Dammit! I wish Hawk would come!" Annette said.

"He has to gather troops, then transport them," Carter explained. "If there are any nearby, it will be faster. But we can't count on it."

"When he comes, he may find us dead, and the place cleared out. The count will escape to continue his mad plan."

"It's a good possibility. We're going to have to help the insurgents. Here's what we'll do," he said, and he related the desperate plan.

Carter and Annette released the cords, and the two big rocks they had found on the dry Kenyan plain swung through two of the floor-to-ceiling panes of window glass.

There was an enormous crash.

Glass shards and slivers sliced like knives into the meeting hall.

The men and women stopped fighting for thirty seconds, shocked, then turned restless to resume the cat-and-mouse game of closing in on the insurgents.

But already Carter and Annette had slipped in unnoticed at the two back doors on opposite sides of the room.

They chose their targets carefully and fired as the two groups of fighters were still trying to reassemble their wits.

Quickly the outnumbered insurgents took in the situation. Across from the two agents, to the left of the count, they had clustered to make their stand. Mr. Justice Stone and several others were wounded. Andrea Sutton appeared unscathed but furious.

The group understood that Annette and Carter were helping them. They fired with renewed vigor from their piecemeal shelters of chairs and tables.

The count's head rose slowly behind the podium, but two of the insurgents saw him and fired. He quickly dropped back. He was like a king with his symbolic throne. He wouldn't give up the podium easily, wouldn't give up the power it represented to him.

Between the small group of fifteen and the two agents, the executioners and soldiers fought. A few realized the two agents were the pincers of a nonexistent outside attack. They shot back, but the accurate aim of Carter and Annette slowly decreased their numbers.

The fighting continued, Carter and Annette picking at the fifty executioners and soldiers one by one, the executioners and soldiers picking at the fifteen insurgents one by one.

Then the roar of helicopters sounded over the reverberations of the meeting hall's gunfire.

A surge of excitement coursed through Carter.

Hawk had received the message and acted. There was a chance for the plan after all.

The soldiers and executioners looked up, puzzled, then

decided it must be the sound of more of their people being transported in.

They resumed their work.

Carter nodded to Annette. She allowed him a dazzling smile through her cold professional mask. She darted back out her door onto the balcony.

Carter snaked around the room, the insurgents' fire occupying the count's men. Through the corners of his eyes, he saw Annette run down the balcony steps. She would meet Hawk's men, tell them the situation, and bring them to the meeting hall.

Carter continued around the hall's perimeter, occasionally having to fight or kill one of the executioners or soldiers.

The Killmaster was closing in on Count Montalban.

As gunshots punctuated the air around them, Count Montalban looked up from his shelter behind the podium and into Nick Carter's eyes. In that one brief moment, understanding passed between them.

In the count's deep-set, arrogant gaze was nobility, age, experience, and belief that what he wanted he could and should have, no matter the cost to others. He lifted his nose as if smelling Carter, hating the odor of a man who saw that in him and wasn't impressed.

They stood frozen during that instant, and then Carter lunged.

Like the wily old jungle fighter he was in Vietnam, the count hunched and streaked across the back of the room, the ivory-handled pistols ready at his sides.

Carter tore after him.

Andrea Sutton shouted a warning.

Her group of insurgents saw the count and fired, leaving a line of holes in the timbered wall.

The count's executioners and soldiers saw Carter and

fired, and the wall splintered and shook with the bullets that could have so easily maimed or killed Carter or the count.

Carter sensed someone behind him, but he couldn't turn as he dashed after the count, running down one corridor after another in the mammoth fort.

Chasing, he turned left and right and left again. Past confused, wandering jury members whose minds had temporarily lost their grip in the violent melee in the meeting hall. Past closed doors behind which frightened members would be cowering or fearfully aiming loaded guns, waiting for the wrong person to enter. Past a startled member who was lugging a heavy suitcase guiltily down the hall, hoping to find an airplane, a Jeep, a camel, anything, to escape.

And then Carter was at a dead end.

A hall of closed doors. No windows. No exit except through the way Carter had entered.

The count had come in here and disappeared.

Carter held the rifle comfortably secure, ready to fire instantly.

Shots, shouts, and the crashing of an invasion by a large force resounded in the distance. The meeting hall. Annette had found Hawk's men.

Carter listened at the first of the six closed doors. Sobbing came from the room, a man's sobbing. The count had repressed the naturalness of tears—just as he had compassion—long ago. That wouldn't be him.

Carter tried the next door. Dead silence. He leaned flat against the wall and, with a singular smooth motion, turned the knob and swung the door open. He ran inside, again flat against the wall. The room was empty. He sighed, walked out, and closed the door.

Behind the third door, music repeated itself, the same measure over and over, too short to be distinguishable. Carter cracked the door and peered in. The jury member was a suicide, hanging from a beamed rafter, his belt cutting into the flesh of his neck, his eyes and tongue bulging purple and black.

At the fourth door, Carter heard a menacing click. He smiled.

Again he flattened himself against the wall, using the same fluid motion to turn the knob and swing open the door.

"You will never leave here alive, Monsieur Carter!" the count growled from inside the room.

Carter remained in the corridor, flat against the wall.

"Come, come, *mon vieux*," the count said, his voice low, enticing. "Little tormenter, little friend. Show yourself!" He smacked his lips together as if calling barnyard animals.

"Just a farmer after all," Carter told him, bemused.

The shotgun blast was instant. The plank corridor wall across from the open door shredded and splintered with the count's impotent revenge. On the edge of madness, the fanatic's temper was the first emotion to go out of control.

The count's angry outburst was all the time the incredibly fast Killmaster needed.

He rolled into the room and crouched, rifle up.

The count was gone. Disappeared again.

Swiftly, Carter took in the empty room. A desk, chair, three guest chairs, file cabinet, wastepaper basket, bulletin board, floor safe, small refrigerator, and mounted wall photographs of the count with animals he'd killed around the world—jaguar, Santa Barbara Channel Islands boar, elephant, gnu, Australia's wild dingo, tiger, an Alaskan grizzly.

The hidden latch was to the left of the desk.

Instantly Carter pressed it. The wall swung open.

Carter darted through onto the balcony and the fresh Kenyan air, the count's automatic secret staircase already rising to tuck itself neatly beneath the overhang.

Directly below on the dusty plain, the count ran, an ivory-handled pistol in one hand, a briefcase in the other. He ran with grace and sureness. There would be a jet at the end of the landing field always waiting for him, ready for immediate takeoff.

A shot rang out as Carter hurdled the balcony rail and leaped down.

"N3!" shouted the gruff voice.

The count glanced over his shoulder, surprised, and bounded on.

Carter knocked the rifle from Lady Andrea Sutton's hand. Tears of frustration and rage streamed down her face.

"The bastard!" she screamed. "He's ruined everything! David's plan! My dream!"

Carter sprinted, gave a mighty leap, and sailed through the air. He tackled the count's legs.

The count rolled and kicked, but Carter held on.

He bashed the briefcase down on Carter's head, but it was a glancing blow—the count was at a poor angle—and Carter hardly felt it.

The count aimed his ivory-handled pistol.

"Watch out, N3!" the gruff voice shouted.

"Hawk!" Carter called, smiling. "What took you so long?"

Carter grabbed the wrist and squeezed with his steely grip.

The count glared, and a cold, evil smile spread across his thin aristocratic lips. The count was strong, and he gloried in it.

Slowly the nobleman rotated his hand so that the pistol was aimed directly at Carter's heart.

Sweating like a glass of Jack Daniel's, Carter forced the hand to continue in the arc. It passed his heart, and the gun was now aimed at the ground.

In a fury, the count dropped the briefcase and compressed

the free hand on Carter's throat.

Hawk's shadow passed over them.

"I'll take him!" Carter told his chief, gritting his teeth, his eyes locked into the count's. "He's mine!"

In Count Montalban he saw the results of thousands of years of greed, ambition, and lies. As long as they could get away with it, greedy, ambitious men would lie, cheat, steal, and kill to build empires of power and wealth. The count was lower than a common pickpocket. He took the advantages given him at birth and turned them against humanity. He was despicable, without the excuse of being poor and ignorant. He'd enslave others for his own profit.

Disgust welled up in Carter.

The Killmaster released the count's legs.

Again the count tried to roll away, his hand still compressing Carter's throat. Carter panted, tried to breathe.

He pried the fingers from his throat.

While he was busy with that, the count again rotated the pistol toward Carter's heart.

"Nick! Be careful!" Lady Andrea Sutton cried, tears still in her voice.

His throat free, Carter jumped up. In one dramatic movement, he yanked the count up by the arm, spun him, then flipped the count up over his back. Still gripping the pistol, the count sailed like an acrobat through the air, headfirst.

As the count landed with a thud on the hard earth, the pistol exploded.

The count screamed.

The shot went through his heart. Blood cascaded out. Astonishment and shock thickened his narrow, aristocratic face. He pressed his hands against the mortal wound, trembling, and still the blood poured.

"Why didn't it work?" he said faintly to no one in particular, except perhaps himself. His lips were already bluing toward inevitable death. "I was right. I could have saved the world. What went wrong?"

"Avarice," Hawk mused.

He stood with Carter and Lady Andrea Sutton on the vast Kenyan plain watching the mop-up operation. With Annette Burden leading, Hawk's tan-suited Kenyan and American troops herded the surviving executioners, soldiers, and jury members out of the meeting room, onto the balcony, and down into a specially designed AXE corral that had just been erected. Others searched through the fort, rounding up the remaining jury members.

"Avarice complicated by certainty," Hawk went on, puffing thoughtfully on his cigar. "There's an old saying in business: When a company's in trouble, to save it you go in and fire the one indispensable man. A company survives and grows on teamwork. So does a country, or a world. No one is indispensable."

Three of Hawk's men with red crosses on their sleeves ran into the meeting hall. Now the troops were carrying out stretchers bearing the wounded. Annette organized them around one of the helicopters.

"Anyone who thinks he's indispensable—or wants to be," Carter said, agreeing with Hawk, "harms the rest of us. Yet we're all absolutely indispensable to ourselves and to our friends and family. But that has to do with self-worth. Unfortunately, indispensability—being right—can be an excuse to go after any goal, good or bad."

"Nick?" Andrea Sutton moved in front of him, staring up at him with soft gray eyes full of pain. "If David . . . or you . . . had been in charge, this . . . none of this . . . would ever have happened. The Rule would have stayed quiet. Small. Done the job no one else would do. Cleaned up the world."

"You don't understand, Andrea," Carter said sadly. "The whole point is that you were wrong from the beginning. Size made it worse, but it didn't change the initial mistake. Vigilantism—taking the law into your hands—is wrong. No civilized country can countenance it."

"But the count turned it all wrong. If David had lived—"

"David was doomed," Carter said patiently. "The magician, the great-grandson of the Kaiser, was in Budapest to kill him. The count had ordered him to kill David as soon as David had finished his assignment. He was following me, couldn't figure out what I was up to. Then David's heart attack saved him the job. The count planned to run the organization himself from the beginning. That's the personality that can develop out of vigilantism."

Her eyes blinked slowly as she digested the news. She frowned.

Off in the distance, Annette was still helping with the wounded, now carrying plasma, bandages, bending her blond head to give a word of assurance.

"But us, Nick . . ." Lady Andrea Sutton moved closer, her breath warm and sweet, her skin smelling of tea roses. "What about us? We still need justice. This is an evil world. We can go on fighting . . . together . . . forever . . ."

Two of Hawk's tan-uniformed troops approached.

"I'm sorry," Carter told Andrea. "I really am."

The men escorted Andrea off to join her comrades in the corral. She looked back over her shoulder, uncomprehending, hurt, lost, but with the beginning again of the old rage. In a few hours she'd be telling herself that she'd been unfairly, unjustly, dealt with by AXE. But it would be empty solace. She'd go to trial, and with the massive evidence against her, she'd be sentenced to prison for a long time by the legal system she claimed was too easy on criminals.

Hawk slapped Carter on the shoulder.

"It was close, N3," he said. "You did a damned fine job."

"There's still work to be done."

"I understand." The AXE chief smiled knowingly. "Go to her. She looks like she could use a hand."

Carter strode across the dry plain, feeling the relief and happiness that came from a difficult mission accomplished, and now, too, feeling smarter, as if he'd learned something vital about life. Annette looked up, eyes bright, innocent of guile. She gave him a glowing smile.

He took the sulfa packets from her hand and pulled her to him. She smelled clean, of sun and healthy work. She wrapped her arms around his neck and raised her lips.

"Kiss me," she said. "I missed you."

He laughed.

"I missed you, too," he said, breathing into her fresh, warm hair. "More than you'll ever know."

DON'T MISS THE NEXT NEW
NICK CARTER SPY THRILLER

THE TARLOV CIPHER

Korydalos Prison was an ominous mass of brown and gray stone squatting on the plain between Athens and the port of Piraeus. At one time the old fortress had probably been the sole piece of architecture for miles around. Now, living just a few miles from the main artery between the city and the port, a thriving community had grown up around it.

The noonday sun boiled fire down on the rutted asphalt of the street separating the main gate from the café where Carter sat sipping a beer. Pedestrians, pushcart vendors, and a steady stream of taxis, bicycles, and motorbikes flowed back and forth across his gaze.

"Another?"

Carter looked up at the waiter and nodded. "One for me and three for my friend. He'll be arriving soon."

The waiter cocked his head across the street. "Korydalos?"

"Yes."

"I'll bring five. I've seen them come out before."

When they arrived, Carter passed the man a generous tip. The waiter had already provided another service by keeping the rear exit of the café clear for their exit.

Carter was a third of the way through the second beer when one of the big steel doors built into the prison wall swung open. A uniformed guard, a civilian, and a second guard stepped out.

The civilian was Demetrius Razik.

He exchanged a few words with the guards and then started across the street toward the café.

Razik had aged; and not well. He was still a huge bear, but now there was a shuffle in his gait. He had shaved his beard but left a long, drooping mustache that failed to hide the perpetual sneer on his lips.

His face looked old, and even though the jaw was wide and the forehead high, the features looked wizened. The skin was full of deep creases, and the eyes peered out from dark, hollow shadows.

In the middle of the street he paused and turned. For several seconds, his shoulders slumped, his head thrown forward like an angry bull, he stared at what had been his home for the last sixteen years.

Suddenly he threw up his arms and a bellow filled the street. "Demetrius Razik, the Greek, says . . . fuck you all!"

He turned on his heel and finished the walk to the café. At Carter's table he drank one of the beers in four quick swallows. With a second in his hand, he gazed around him, inhaling the sights, the sounds, and the smells of freedom.

He drank the second beer like the first, sat down, and thrust his hand toward Carter.

"You look as old as I feel, American. How is the spy business?"

"Booming," Carter replied, taking the hand.

"Good. Where is the rest of what I asked for?"

Razik had requested beer, a gun, and a woman on his release. Carter slipped a Mauser from his belt and passed it under the table. Razik took it and slipped it into his belt beneath his shirt.

"And the woman?"

"She will have to wait, Razik."

"Why?"

"Because I think that somewhere out there on the street there are several people who are about to try and kill you."

"Then why didn't you have me come out at night, by a private gate?" He started on the last beer.

"Because I want you in my debt when I save your lousy skin."

The big head went back and a roar of laughter filled the café. "American, you are the same heartless bastard I knew and loved long ago!" He raised his beer in a salute, then drained it.

In short, clipped sentences Carter laid down the ground rules. He was in charge from here on in, and Razik would do what he was told.

"Agreed. All I want is my money."

"Half is already on deposit." He handed Razik a Swiss passbook.

The other man inspected it, nodded, and slipped it into his pocket. "And now?"

"Now we get the hell out of here."

The Killmaster led the way through the café. The alley behind the rear exit was empty.

"This way!"

They had barely gotten a hundred yards from the mouth of the alley toward the village square when Carter sensed them closing in.

He spoke to Razik from the side of his mouth. "At the edge of the square, a man on a motorcycle will block our path.

Two more will come up behind us.''

"Yes.''

"You take out the two behind us. I'll get the one in front.''

"Shoot them . . . in broad daylight?''

"That's right,'' Carter replied. "Then we run like hell across the square.''

"Then what?''

"Four men in a white Mercedes will wrestle us into the car. Don't fight them.''

"Yours?''

"Yes.''

"I don't get it.''

"You will,'' Carter said and grinned.

They were practically into the square when Carter saw them. Three men, dressed like tourists, moved toward them from the center fountain. Two more were converging from the mouth of an alley to their right, and two from the left.

They all had bull necks, broad, Slavic faces, and menace in their eyes. Unlike the two locals on Mykonos, these men knew what they were doing and they moved with purpose. Also, there wasn't a Greek in the bunch.

Carter smiled with satisfaction. Of the seven, he didn't recognize a single face that matched one of the four who had come after him and Darva outside the restaurant near Astir.

Then they came, seemingly out of nowhere. The sound of the big motorcycles was deafening in the square. Carter didn't turn. He was counting on Razik to keep track of the two he could hear coming up behind them.

Then Carter saw the source of the sound in front of them. All in black, including helmet and visor, came a rider on a big BMW. He looked like something out of hell as he veered around a car, spotted Carter, and did a broadside toward the Killmaster.

Whether by accident or pure riding genius on the rider's

part, he practically slid the big bike right into Carter's legs. The rider came off his machine in a roll. When he came up to his knees, his hands were full of .45.

"Now!" Carter yelled, dropping to one knee and filling his hand with Wilhelmina. He sensed rather than saw Razik do the same right beside him, facing their rear.

"You're sure?" the Greek said.

"I'm sure," the Killmaster growled.

Razik's Mauser sounded like a cannon in the square. Carter's shots from Wilhelmina chimed in.

The rider in front of him practically did a back flip, landing spread-eagle on his belly.

A quick glance told Carter that the two helmeted riders had been dispatched as well by Razik.

The crowd in the square had been starting to mass when it all started. Probably bloodlust, sensing the beginnings of a good fight.

At the sight of the guns, they had held back. When the firing started, they began to run.

Now all was chaos and pandemonium.

The men who had been closing in on them had no choice but to fall back as well.

"Let's go!" Carter bellowed.

He fired into the air as they ran. Razik, following Carter's lead, did the same. The crowd parted in front of them, and they passed through like a hot knife through butter.

In less than a block, a big white Mercedes sedan shot from a side street and braked.

"Them?" Razik panted.

"Them," Carter hissed, not slowing his pace.

The Mercedes was rocking directly in front of them when the doors opened and four figures in dark coveralls, with ski masks over their heads, spilled out.

Two of them went to their knees and surveyed the crowd

with the ugly snouts of Uzi submachine guns.

The third and fourth grabbed Carter and Razik by the backs of their necks. At the same time, they did their best to grind the muzzles of a couple of Berettas into their ears.

"In the car, in the car!" they both screamed in unison.

Carter let himself be propelled forward. He sailed through an open door and landed on the floor of the back seat. Two seconds later, Razik was lying across him and the car doors slammed. Tires squealed and they were on their way.

The whole thing had taken less than half a minute.

"You sure the lads on the bikes were ours?" Razik panted.

"I'm sure," Carter replied.

"Then why did we waste them?"

"We didn't." The Killmaster smiled. "Blanks. You don't think I'd trust you with real ammunition, do you?"

—From *THE TARLOV CIPHER*
A New Nick Carter Spy Thriller
From Charter in December 1985